A MANSION WITH MANY ROOMS: A COLLECTION OF SHORT STORIES AND POEMS.

leilahpublications.com Tempe AZ USA 85281

Retailers and independent sellers to order wholesale trade:
(800) 937-8000 Ingram Content Group Inc.
One Ingram Blvd.
La Vergne, TN 37086

Introduction.

In the course of my career as a writer and musician, ideas for short stories and poems would rise in my imagination from time to time. My first novel, "A Quantum Hijra," was the result of the idea for a short story I had while waiting in line at a grocery store (ironically, in the course of writing the book, that original story was edited out, and no longer exists in any form. I doubt I could reproduce it if I tried).

The reader will note that, as is the case of most writers, I write based on my personal experience. I am a Muslim / Sufi, a musician, and a number of other things. My fiction and poetry will forever be reflective of this.

As with my music, I divide my efforts into two polar opposites: artistic and business. The latter is simply an honest effort to gain fair and just financial remuneration for the production of a work of value. The former is a bit more multi-faceted. I see my creations as a form of yoga or kung fu: something akin to a spiritual discipline. Furthermore, I see it as a service to humanity. There have been times people read my writing (or heard my music) and derived some personal benefit from it. These reports gratify me, and inspire me to work harder to perfect my craft.

It is my wish that the reader will find something within my humble efforts beyond mere entertainment.

Yunus and his Wife.

It was raining when I first noticed Yunus.

Friday Jumma prayers at the mosque had just ended. It was a pleasant, but unremarkable service. As always, the brothers and sisters were congregating outside the mosque, talking, selling their wares. Everyone was holding umbrellas, or huddled under eaves or awnings of buildings. It really wasn't raining that hard, come to think of it. But it was a cold, damp rain that seemed to penetrate everything.

There was a man off to the side. He was about my height, thin, shabbily dressed, and carrying a large backpack. His stringy red hair hung in his face. He spoke to nobody and nobody spoke to him. He stood there with his prayer beads, a haunted, distracted look in his deep green eyes.

People seemed to avoid him, the way people avoid the homeless or insane. His appearance, while not attractive, was nonetheless at least clean. I couldn't be sure, but he seemed in acceptable health. His shoes – for a man's shoes speak volumes – were in good condition, although inexpensive and seemed to have been chosen to dissuade attention. He was, as I'd heard, a recluse. Many people thought he was crazy. He rarely spoke to anyone, and while he was never rude or antagonistic, he kept people at arm's length. The company of people seemed to repel him.

His name was Yunus.

Thinking back on it now, I can't figure out why he would single me out to socialize with, to make, after a fashion, a friend. Perhaps he needed some kind of human contact. Or maybe the act of sharing his personal secrets with me was a confession. You will read this story with the same incredulity that Yunus' story unfolded in front of me as I got to know him. It is a truly bizarre story, and you may find it disturbing. But part of what makes it disturbing is that Yunus' life shows us truths that we are not comfortable to admit.

That afternoon, I strolled about outside the mosque. People were selling the kind of items one sees outside a mosque; Islamic books and videos, incense and perfumes, clothing, food, and the like. I was contemplating buying a bean pie. Deciding not to, I turned around, and Yunus was standing directly in front of me, staring me in the eye.

Normally, when a reputed crazy person singles you out for eye contact, this could be cause for concern. However, my initial adrenaline rush was subdued by the look in his eyes. It was not the kind of aggressive challenge some lunatics with an attitude would show. This was curiosity.

"Who are you?" He said, simply. At that moment, I remembered the passage of Alice's Adventures in Wonderland, where Alice met the Caterpillar. Well, unlike Alice, I knew who I was. I introduced myself. "Asalaam alaikum. My name is Jamal Khan."

He stared at me for a long moment. His eyes seemed to be focusing on a point somewhere behind the space between my eyes; an effect I (and anyone else he met) found disturbing. "Wa alaikum asalaam. I'm Yunus." he said finally, a touch of an Irish brogue in his voice. I held out my hand to shake his. He looked at it for a second, as if he had no idea what I was doing. Finally, he shook my hand. The palms were rough and calloused, and dry.

He looked at me again; focusing beyond my eyes, and said "You're hungry." This was not a question. And then I realized that I was very hungry. He said, "Let's eat something that our bodies will find agreeable."

I agreed, but his choice of words was a little strange. He walked toward a restaurant, a Muslim owned place across the street from where we were. I followed, and we went in and sat down at a table in a secluded corner.

The waitress, a pretty young African American woman in a hijab brought us menus and glasses of water. I was, at this point, resigned to the fate of picking up the check. Yunus kept his backpack next to him, seeming to refuse to let it out of his sight, and wanting always some physical contact with it, and examined the menu intently, and at one point, asked the waitress where they purchased their meat. She looked at him as if he was crazy (and I'm sure she had already formulated an opinion about him) and said she wasn't sure. "Well, find out for me, please." Yunus said. Nonplussed, the waitress went to speak to the manager.

The manager came to us and asked if there was a problem. By now, I was sure there was going to be a scene, and regretted not walking away after being asked who I was. However, Yunus simply asked again where they purchased their meat. The manager gave him the name of the distributor, and Yunus smiled and said "By Allah! By Allah! You have made a wise choice, my brother! I'm so happy!" He looked as if he would begin weeping with joy, and the manager looked as if he couldn't make up his mind to smile or kick him out. He looked at me a moment, and said something that I supposed meant he was happy that we were all happy. Then he walked away and spoke briefly to the waitress, looking at us (I looked back, and discreetly shrugged my shoulders) and went about his business. For a long while, Yunus stared at his glass of water, as if it were a TV set with an engrossing program on.

The waitress returned and took our orders. Yunus ordered a turkey burger with fries. I ordered a salad. Yunus ate without saying a word. When the check came, Yunus, to my surprise, grabbed it, and pulled a roll of money out of his pocket the size of my fist. Nothing in his appearance or behavior would lead me to believe he had any money. I thanked him for the meal. He responded only with a glance and a half smile.

We left the restaurant, and Yunus started walking. He looked back at me as if to say "Are you coming, or not?" I followed him.

After three blocks, I said, "Where are we going?" He said "For tea." He didn't break his stride. I hurried to catch up to him and asked, "Where are we having tea?" He looked at me intently, and said "Home."

"I beg your pardon?"

"Home. Me home."

He said this so matter of fact that I almost couldn't resist him. His manner held me in an irresistible momentum.

We came to a nondescript apartment building, and I followed him inside. The building was old, and we climbed creaky wood stairs to the top floor. His door was in a dark corner of the hall, and there was no number or any marking on it. Stepping inside, he places his backpack on an ottoman that dominated one of the corners of the room. I'd not known what to expect when I walked in. The one room studio apartment was the single most Spartan dwelling place I'd ever laid eyes on. The entire furnishing consisted of a small refrigerator with a hot plate on top of it, a cupboard above an old sink, a closet, a bathroom, a mattress and box spring and mattress covered with a few blankets and a pillow, a chair, a table with candles and a lamp on it, a pile of about three dozen books and some CDs near the bed, a boom box, and the ottoman I mentioned; which had a large incense burner under it. Nothing else.

But the walls, the walls were completely covered in designs. Patterns, colors, and vague suggestions of images of faces and animals done in paint, markers, even what looked like pen and ink! Some of it was meticulously carved into the plaster of the walls, and filled in with color. Some of it looked like calligraphy; but it was not a script I could identify. The intricacy was not to be believed. It even covered the ceiling. One saw this and wondered what kind of mind could have the patient obsession to do such a thing.

Anyone who saw it would believe it to be the home of a madman. And of course, Yunus' reputation was not that of a well-adjusted person. Now, I was in the midst of his world.

The incense burner under the ottoman was something that demands some mention. First, this is a strange place to put an incense burner. It was a large elaborately designed piece, of Chinese design. Residue was caked around its top. But it was the smell that was truly noticeable; whatever he burned in it was unlike anything I'd ever smelled before. And, being a Muslim, I was familiar with incense.

"Please, make yourself comfortable" he said, indicating the chair near the window. I sat down. The chair, like everything else in the place, was old and worn. But it was quite comfortable.

Sunlight was fading and the sky was darkening. He pulled out a prayer rug from the closet, made the call to prayer, and motioned for me to lead the prayer. We made prayer as the room became darker and darker.

After prayer, he lit the candles on his table. The candles were in a large metal bowl that he allowed the wax to drip into and at times spill over onto the table. I would have preferred the lamp; because the candle light cast strange and unearthly shadows on the weird artwork on his walls.

Yunus then apologized for not making the tea he'd promised. He turned on his radio, and went to his makeshift kitchenette. As he put the water on, "Strange Relationship" by (the artist formerly known as) Prince came on. Yunus stopped what he was doing, and stared at the radio. As the song drew to a close, he laughed hysterically. "What's so funny?" I asked cautiously, not sure I wanted to know the answer. "The song! It reminds me of my wife!" Yunus said, amidst more cackling laughter. I didn't know what to make if this. Yunus was married? There was no indication that he lived with her. Which was not surprising, because I couldn't imagine a woman wanting to live the way Yunus apparently enjoyed living.

"You seem like a good man," Yunus said when the tea was ready, handing me a cup. "You seem like the kind of person who would not judge a situation unless he had all the facts. Most people see a part of me, a part of what my life is, and they jump to hasty conclusions. The invent lies about me! Well, let them. I just want to share the truth about my life with another human being. Nobody but you ever gave me the chance to do this."

This sudden burst of honesty and candor was a bit startling. I knew that it came from a raw emotional place. He had apparently had little real human contact. Now, I was really curious about where this was going to lead. Was he an emotional cripple of some kind who can't make real social contact? Someone who'd had a bad experience and whose mind never recovered? And what will his presence, and confession, bring to my life?

"But before I get to that, tell me about yourself!" he said invitingly, cheerfully.

I was not anxious to let him know much about myself. He was the kind of person who could (or so it appeared) see inside you, and at the same time, was completely disconnected from his surroundings. Well, I ended up talking about myself a while. I told him of my family life (never mentioning any names – and he never asked), my education, and my job as a data processor for an insurance company. He would occasionally punctuate my monologue with questions. But all along, he gave me the impression that the whole act of conversation was something completely foreign to him. I was reminded of a passage in Thomas Harris' book "Red Dragon" where the serial killer Dollarhyde met the blind woman. He finally realized that he was engaging in conversation with another human being. Something he'd never really done before. This is how Yunus reacted; as if our talk was an entirely new experience for him.

He had been sitting cross-legged on his bed the whole time. Suddenly, he got up, turned off the music (he'd been playing a CD: "Silk Road" by Kitaro) and spread out the prayer rug. This time, he led prayer. His voice reciting Qur'an was quite compelling; but in a manner that didn't resemble anything I'd ever heard before. Perhaps it was his Irish accent. His choice of Qur'anic verses was interesting: 15:27 and 27:39.

After prayer, he sat on the floor. I sat again on the chair, and was trying to think of a way to make a graceful exit.

"Now, you will hear my story." he said. When he began his story, the light from his candles suddenly became a little brighter.

Or so I thought. His Irish brogue became thicker. And his eyes shined out of the darkness of the room like a cat's eyes reflecting whatever light catches it.

"I came from Belfast, Ireland. My family moved to America when I was 15. I grew up wanting to be an engineer. I was good at math. When I was 22, I left college and joined the air force. They paid for my education, and I got to travel quite a bit. The whole time, I didn't join the others in carousing, drinking, and whatever. I stayed on the base, and saved me money. Strange thing for an Irishman, I know! My race is known for its love of drink

"After about six years, I was in an accident. It was a plane crash in Germany. I was injured. My left leg was shattered. I spent two years in rehabilitation, and got an honorable discharge. When I could walk again, I spent some years traveling. I went everywhere. About ten years ago, I converted to Islam while in India. I was working for a while as a consultant for an engineering firm. I took me Shahada; but I was never really one of these people who went overboard spouting me mouth off about it. It was more of a private thing betwixt Allah and me. I got tired real fast of people looking at me, a white Muslim convert, like I was some kind of 'special' Muslim, some kind of curiosity on display, or any body's pride and joy – or target of hate. I never cared a rat's bottom what people thought of me, Muslim or non-Muslim! I was only interested in Allah, and my own soul. They can take the rest of that rigmarole and stuff it!

"During this time, I spent several years learning to play the saragni from an Ustad. That's what they call a master musician; 'Ustad.' It's like a title or something. Eventually, I quit me job. I really didn't like it; I just did it to save money, and concentrated on music.

"But none of this is telling you anything about my wife, is it? I could see you were interested in her! Boy, you perked right up when I mentioned her, you did! Well, I tell you, she's shy, and not many people ever see her."

"Yunus," I began cautiously, "I hope I hadn't offended you when you mentioned your wife. I just,,,"

He got up, went to his incense burner, and lit some incense. That strange scent filled the air. Then, he opened the bag on the ottoman, and pulled his sarangi from it. He sat down on his bed, and held the instrument. "You didn't think I was married," he said. "You think I'm crazy and no woman would want me. It's OK, Haki. I'm not angry. I get this sort of thing all the time. I'm not supposed to have money or be able to do anything but beg for chump change and piss me pants!"

I could say nothing.

"Hey, it's OK. Don't you fret, now. Anyway, I stayed in India a number of years. I loved the sarangi. I spent hours, days playing it. I did seven chillas in one year. You know what a chilla is? It's when you lock yourself away and do nothing for X number of days but play. I got good. I did a few private concerts here and there. But I didn't want to be a professional musician. I'm not exactly what you'd call a 'people person,' you see.

"After a while, the travel bug hit me. I packed up and left India. I roamed around. Eventually I ended up in Egypt. That's when something happened that changed me life forever.

"As I said, I was in Egypt. I actually didn't like it there. Mind you, the people were great, and I enjoyed seeing the pyramids and the Valley of the Kings and whatnot. It's the police and the government I hated. They're all a bunch of Nancy Boys with guns if you ask me! I mean, they harassed me several times! And for what? Because I'm a Celtic Muslim with an Indian instrument traveling on his own? It's not like I'll be strapping C4 to me bum to go blow up the Sphinx or the Holy See's outhouses, for pity's sake!

"One night during Ramadan I was in a desert. It may have been Laylatul Qadr, but I'm not sure. Nobody is. You ever been in a desert at night?"

I nodded my head yes.

"Quite a scene, isn't it? Most people think it's hot all the time. But it gets cold, don't it? And the moon! The moon is like, looking at you with its light. You see it, and it sees you. And Paul Bowles was right; the sky is sheltering. Like a blanket the size of all of heaven!

"I had me sarangi with me. I always have it with me. It never leaves me side. Anyway, I'd just finished making prayerul tarawih alone on the cold sand. I pulled me saragni out of the bag I carry it in, and started to play. I was improvising something, mixing ragas, and things I heard in Arab music. I have a pretty good ear, you see.

"I was playing a long time. The music seemed to fill up the whole world. I always play me best when I'm alone. And I was alone. I thought I was alone,,,,,"

Yunus paused, and his downcast face seemed to recollect a time that took an effort to speak about, or even to endure its memory.

"I was playing me music,, 'MY' music, you understand, and I saw a leopard. Now, this worried me. They don't teach you how to defend yourself from wild animals in the Air Force Corps of Engineers! I had no weapon. Nothing but me saragni. But this leopard just stood there. Not growling or anything. And I'd just kept playing. It was all I could do. Maybe the music has charms to sooth the savage beast, or whatever that's supposed to be. Then a wind came up, kicked up a bunch of sand. For a moment I couldn't see the leopard, and I got worried, because maybe it would come up out of nowhere and attack me.

"But then, the leopard was gone, and a woman was standing there!

"You can't imagine how surprised I was! I stopped playing for a moment. I was worried that the leopard would come out and attack her. But she walked up to me and stood about three meters from me. She was wearing a purple alba. Her hair was partly visible, and her face was uncovered. She was a beautiful Arab girl. About 22, petite, with dark skin, full red lips, and long thick hair. Her eyes,,, her eyes, man, they were like black diamonds shining out of the hieroglyphics on an ancient shrine. Never seen the like before. So beautiful.

"She came a little closer and sat down. She stared at me said 'Asalaam alaikum.' I returned the salaam; and I tell you, me voice cracked a bit!

"Then she said 'I love you.'

"Just then, another wind came up. It blew sand all over the place, and her alba was flying all over. I covered me eyes, I couldn't see, and then when the wind stopped, she was gone! There was a rose on the ground where she was sitting. I picked it up, and put it in me bag.

"Now, I never really knew much about this sort of thing. I remember me grandmother telling me stories about 'The Little People', and hearing about the Arabian Nights and flying carpets and the like. But this was something new to me. I was suddenly very cold. I made dhikr has hard as I could; but the more I made it, the stronger the feeling that I wasn't alone.

"I had some dates, a couple of samosas, and a bottle of water with me. I had me sahur, and then made the Fajr prayer. Just after the sun was up, I walked back to the place where I was staying, and went to sleep. Now, I was a little scared to go to sleep. But I slept well.

"The next day, I got a sudden urge to leave the country. I packed me bag, and booked a flight to Tangiers. When I got there and got settled in, I tried to find out about the mountains. I wanted to find a place where I could be alone with nature. I spend about a week exploring the mountains. I met some musicians and played with them in their village. Smoked a lot of hashish with them too. They ended up giving me a good size brick of it. I still have some. Managed to get it back here to the states with no trouble. You want to have a smoke?"

"No thanks." I said. The place, his persona, and the story he was telling me were enough without a head full of hashish. "Please, continue."

"Well, let me know if you change your mind. Don't be shy. Now, where was I? Oh yes. One night when I was wandering about the mountains, I found a cave. I built a fire in it, and sat and played me sarangi. Then I saw something out of the corner of me eye. Something moving. Well, this could be anything; or it could just be that hashish.

"I looked again, and it was the Arab girl I'd seen in Egypt! Still in the purple alba, and still beautiful. She stood against the wall of the cave. I stopped playing. By now, I knew she was a djinn. She looked at me with the most intense look of love and longing and said 'I love you, Yunus." She knew me name! 'Don't be scared,' she said. 'I won't hurt you. You came to my desert with your lovely music. The sound you were giving to the desert night made me fall in love with you.'

"Well, I was still scared out of me wits! Ready to mess me trousers, I was. I almost ran away. But then she did something that stopped me dead in me tracks. She cried. Now, she didn't go to pieces howling or anything. But tears were coming from her eyes, her beautiful eyes. She seemed to know exactly what I was feeling. And she seemed to feel bad that she was hurting me and scaring me. I could feel it; I could feel what she was feeling. We were communicating without words.

"But what kind of a thing would it be to have a djinn hanging about? Could I marry her? How would me Mum take to her? What about her Mum?"

Just then, Yunus began to draw the bow across the strings of his sarangi. A quiet single drone hung gently in the air.

"Well, I didn't know what to do, or what to say. Just then, she said 'I've been alone my whole life. I'm old, much older than you can know. I've never known a friend. I had no love. I hide from everyone and everything. I stayed in that desert for a thousand years. I made prayer and made dhikr; but my people left me to my solitude. I was so lonely; I never thought I could feel anything else. Your music was the only beautiful thing anyone ever gave me. You're more beautiful to me than any other of the Children of Adam I ever saw in all the long centuries.'

"I didn't know what to say to this. But I tell you this, I finally realized that I was just as lonely as she was. It seemed like we'd both found kindred spirits. Do you see? We understood each other!"

He started to play a little. He was marvelous! This shabby, crazy man was a master musician! A virtuoso hiding in the shadows! He spoke in between melodies, all the while continuing the drone on the instrument.

"Then I asked her name. She said 'In all the long centuries, I never told anyone of the Children of Adam my name. My name is Azazadha. My name is Azazadha.'

"We stayed in the cave and talked all night. I told her about me life, and she told me about hers. She told me things about the world of the djinn that most human beings don't know, and even less have the strength to endure. Secrets, man! Things that you wouldn't believe! Well! Morning came, and we made prayer together. And afterwards, she recited Ayatul Kursi! That proved that she wasn't a shaitaheen, at least.

"The next night I returned to the cave. I played me music for her, and she came. I told her that I couldn't get her out of me mind. She said she wanted only me. She said "I have waited a thousand years for you." We decided to get married. Now, this is easier said than done, mind you! We had a hard time finding witnesses! But then I found an old Sheikh in Morocco, and she found someone among her people.

"We were happy together. We still are. But we were rejected by our people. I had to leave the village where I was staying, because it was known that me wife was a djinn, and people thought I would put a curse on them. Azazadha's people didn't much like me either. You'd be surprised how many of the djinn are afraid of us! So I traveled wherever I could, and Azazadha traveled with me. We've been together ever since."

He continued to improvise his music. I started to protest, and told him that most scholars of Shari'ah agreed that it is forbidden to marry a djinn. I told him that the Qur'an tells us to marry from among our own kind. He ignored me, all the while engrossed in that weird music he was playing. It was beautiful, but had an otherworldly quality; which I suppose he was right at home with. I was having a hard time concentrating on what I wanted to tell him. Now, it gives me no pleasure to tell someone he's doing something bad. But this was just too much for me.

The chair that I sat in was to the right of the ottoman I'd mentioned earlier. The incense was still burning, and the smoke was getting a little thick. I would occasionally see movements out of the corner of my eye, but I put that down to the strange artwork on the walls and the shadows cast by the candlelight.

Then I turned and looked at the ottoman. Why I did, I don't know. But to my utter astonishment, a woman was sitting there! She was wearing a purple alba, and was exactly as Yunus described her, except she had a transparent veil over the lower part of her face. My skin shivered, my heart raced, and my breath stopped. I couldn't move. To say I was scared was one thing. But unless you have seen a djinn, you, my dear respected reader, cannot know what a shock the sight of a djinn is to the normal senses of a human being. Because there is intelligence, an awareness and sentience that does not in any way resemble our own. Our minds immediately try to reject it; but can't – and all we're left with is fear.

Yunus said "Jamal, this is my wife, Azazadha." The woman gently said "Asalaam alaikum." The voice was a woman's voice, and held no hint of threat; but the sound she made could not have been produced by flesh. I tried to speak to return the greeting, but couldn't; so I merely nodded. Yunus added "She always comes when I play me sarangi."

She sat there, motionless, staring at me with eyes that did not blink. What thoughts were hiding behind those unearthly eyes, I wondered? What did she see when she looked at me? Did she know what I was seeing? She made a strange soundless flowing movement – I couldn't see her legs, of course – toward Yunus, and kissed him on the cheek as tenderly as I'd ever seen a wife kiss her husband. The room seemed to be saturated with an intense love they shared between them – or was it merely desire?

With Yunus' music playing in the background, she spoke.

"Jamal, son of Adam" she began (what a strange way of addressing me!) "You think our union is strange and unnatural.

You sought refuge in what you think you know of Qur'an. Yunus and I are, indeed, 'among ourselves.' Ours is a love that the ignorant reject. We were rejected with injustice from our people, and we have only each other. Nothing can exist outside Allah, and nothing happens that Allah does not permit. The beauty of the worlds is Allah's permutations. All differences of manifestation are derived from Allah's love of Himself. Majesty and Beauty are attributes of Allah; and the awe and intimacy that creation experiences in perceiving this is the effect of those attributes. Nothing becomes the object of awe and intimacy because nothing exists except Allah. The effect is the same as the attribute, and the attribute is no different from the object. There is nothing that exists except the Divine Presence in His Essence, His Attribute, and His Acts. This is why our love is not forbidden by any except the ignorant! There is nothing else except the Lover and the Beloved!"

I was speechless. What do you say to that, and in such a setting?

"That's me girl!" Yunus said, and she giggled a little, an unnerving sound. All the while, Yunus continued to play. In retrospect, it seemed that his music was in sync with Azazadha's words, or perhaps he was responding to her.

Just then, she said something to Yunus in a strange, liquid language. Allah knows, but I may have heard a sample of the language of the djinns. He started to play faster and more intricate melodies, slashing at the strings of his sarangi with wild abandon. If he had chosen to perform in public, he'd be hailed a genius! A wind seemed to stir, and the candlelight flickered. Suddenly, the music came to an abrupt halt, the candles went out, and, except for the light from a street lamp, we were in darkness.

Yunus got up and turned on the lamp. Azazadha was gone. But I could still feel a third presence in the room.

"Jamal," Yunus began "Our visit is over. You've seen enough for one night, I think, and I don't want to blow your mind any more than it already is! I'm sorry I had to do this the way I did. Azazadha likes you, I think! We'd discussed me sharing our company with another human. You made her feel quite comfortable. She's kind of shy, you see. Thank you, me brother, for letting me share this. I needed to do this for a long time." He got up, and handed me my coat. He walked me to the front door of the building.

"I need to spend some 'quality time' with Azazadha. And tonight is our night for intimacy. Must be a good husband now, mustn't I?" he said with a wink.

I really didn't want to think about it.

"Me brother," he said "You had yourself a time tonight, I know. And I'm grateful that you let me unburden me self. Now, I'm not ashamed; but we all need to reach out sometimes. But Jamal, be careful who you tell this tale to, if you ever decide to speak of it. Most people won't take to it as well as you did! Me, I can handle me self; and Azazadha is perfectly safe from these rapscallions!"

We shook hands, exchanged salaams; and I walked out.

I've given a lot of thought to what happened that night.

There is a general consensus among most scholars of Shari'ah that it is forbidden – or at least inadvisable – for a human and a djinn to marry. There are a lot of very good reasons for this, and I would not argue. They are so very different from us. How do you live with one? What kind of society do they have and how would a human fit into it? Is Azazadha truly a Muslim djinn, or a kaffir shaitaheen intent upon seducing a human she'd become infatuated with? What will happen if they have children? What offspring does such a union produce? How will it be raised, and what world will it live in?

I prefer not to give an opinion one way or another. Let Allah be their judge. What I saw – what I believed I saw - were two lonely misfits who were too shy to communicate with anyone, and who'd found solace in each other. They were both loners in their own worlds who couldn't adapt to their environment – or simply didn't know how. So they created their own world wherein there is only room for them and Allah. The effect on Yunus' life with this woman djinn is difficult to measure, as I have no way to know what he was like before their meeting. To be sure, he is an eccentric man, an oddball. His appearance would, however, occasionally give evidence of a vast intelligence, imagination, and independent spirit that he guarded jealously. I imagine living with a djiin, no matter how well intentioned that djinn may be, would have an effect on anyone. It's possible that the marriage is destroying him, exiling him from his family, from normal human contact, and is slowly shattering his already fragile sanity. Surely, apart from his narrative, his "people skills" are awful. He really doesn't understand inter-human relations at all, and probably never did.

And it occurred to me that the closer Azazadha came to Yunus, the more "normal" his behavior became. I cannot explain this; but in retrospect, it was quite noticeable.

I imagine that it may have been the same with Azazadha. Perhaps her marriage to Yunus the human has changed her, and caused effects on her djinn nature. But this is speculation; I don't know anything about djinn or their world, and I really don't want to know. Meeting Azazadha was as close to it as I ever want to get. Allah is best to know.

As for their fate, I must also place this in Allah's merciful keeping. Yunus disappeared. His apartment was found vacated, empty except for that weird artwork that covered the walls. No trace of the artwork remains; the landlord sanded, spackled, and painted over it before renting the place to someone else. This was over ten years ago. Nobody at the mosque ever saw him again. And neither have I.

Bad Neighborhood

A man came up to me and asked me "Where do you live?" I told him, "I live just outside of Hell".

"What? Impossible!" He retorted.

"Yes, it's true. I live just outside of Hell.

"Where I live, there is great confusion. It is populated by terrible demons! They make gods out of everything their vanity dictates. They are dazzled by images of whatever appeals to their egos, and then they recreate them in material form and worship them. Some force others to worship the false gods the made. They do this by threatening or tormenting them; or by seducing them with alluring speech and images.

"Others speak with beautiful words. They lie and make the lie sound believable; and many do. Most of those who believe these lies are liars themselves. After a while, there are so many lies that nobody knows the truth they were trying to cover up! The lies choke their very throats, until they can't speak a word of truth.

"Some are consumed with a mad desire to be gods. They will stop at nothing to become an 'idol'.

"Many of them destroy everything they come in contact with. Like a virus, they consume every natural resource and leave nothing but waste and corruption. With great delight, they commit the most unspeakable crimes; breeding more horrors than a man's mind can comprehend. They practice perversions of the body, mind, and spirit with an exacting scientific skill.

"The Seven Poisons of the soul have become monuments and institutions. Shaitan rules there with an iron hand. His djinn work tirelessly to accomplish his insane plan. His poisons are effective tools he uses to keep his promise.

"There are human beings there. Some are hopelessly lost. They are trapped in the worship of false gods: and have even created their own false gods so demented as to rival the ones the Shaitaheen made! It's hard to tell them from the djinn!

"Some want to leave, but they can't. They are weak and have no guidance, and they know nothing but Hell. They carry Hell in their hearts and don't know it!

"Some are being guided out of Hell. It's a very difficult task! There are many pitfalls and errors of judgment that hinder the path. Viscous djinn lay in wait at every step to seduce with alluring images; or to rend at the brain, heart, or genitals! They try to abandon the Hell they carry; but Hell doesn't want to be abandoned!

"I don't like it there! I am trying to find the way out! I want Unity and only have separation! Can you help?"

The man looked at me and said "Have you been to a Church?"

I said "That's where many of the false gods live!"

He said "Have you tried speaking to a doctor?"
I said "Futility and more futility!"

He said "What TV shows do you watch?"

I said "None! I'd just as soon drink raw sewage".

He said "Who did you vote for?"

I realized that he was lost too. He must live down the block from me. And so I said "Farewell".

He said "But what about Hell?"

I said "You'll have no trouble finding it. It's not far".

The Sacrificial Virgin

Verdant arms envelope our weary hearts.

A symphony of aromas of the lost Garden emanate from her skin;

Shaming the jasmine and the rose.

Liquid eyes shine like black diamonds of kindness, piercing the breast
from a dark warm night sky.

Lips like sweet fruit speak soft poetry, an invitation to

shared secrets.

Solomon's mountains of myrrh and hills of frankincense lay open to my
wishes.

Sunlight longing to caress bodies cloistered too long within artificial
temples of empty hearts,

Wind asking to play with our hair.

I melt, a seeker of Delectable Sweetness,

In love's garden of flavorful flora,

My heart, a sorbet of rainbow essences,

Wherein love is an absurd, fragile confection of pleasure and pain, and
all that is in between.

The moon rises above the virgin desert;

As this sacred caravansari travels its Sacred Drift.

She passed from the stone cold dusk of the stairs of gold and rose.

She entered the musician's room.

The musician's room was austere and elegant.

The floor was covered in leopard skins.

An ambergris and musk perfume of indescribable sweetness caressed the

currents of the air;

Shamed only by the aroma of her skin.

At its center a Lamp hung with no suspension or fuel needed;

Its Light burns forever.

And round it revolves the hieroglyphics of an ancient dream.

She lifts her amethyst eyelids

Gleaming like a miraculous mist.

Grey shadows played upon the blue sky.

The sunrise kissed the wisdom of her innocence.

The loveliest arms in all the world

Blushed from the lilac bed.

The Rose unfolds and swallows the Midnight Sun.

Shining from her smooth brow like a young star at its birth.

Pale flames canopied the approaching night.

Sad violets that bound the maiden lay sacrificed.

Behold! The wealth of the heart is written in the face of the wild and innocent!

I have beheld the essence of the rose;

Union has brought closer the Lover, HU, Whom our hearts seek:

The dark eyed houris of Paradise shall come as little surprise.

An Iron Tower upon an Unsound Foundation, and a Fortress Built upon a Mountain.

Malik was on his way to the mosque. His friend Mujedid was giving a talk. This was something he wouldn't miss for anything.

He accidentally bumped into a man on the sidewalk. "Excuse me" Malik said. The man shot him a penetrating glare, and left without a word, as if Malik was not worth wasting speech upon. Malik suddenly felt cold. He knew something about the man was wrong.

The man's name was Morris Silverstein.

Morris Silverstein was a wealthy 42 year old former intelligence officer for the USMC who presently worked in international finances. It was late at night when he got the message to attend the meeting. He was at home, a luxury apartment in Manhattan with Spartan furnishings, when a man knocked on his door. Silverstein was surprised and angered to find that his visitor had walked through the security system of his building as if it didn't exist. The man handed him an envelope and disappeared without a word. Silverstein closed the door, sat down and opened the envelope. It read:

Dear Mr. Silverstein,

Your presence is required at a meeting to take place on October 13th, 8:00 P.M. Transportation will be provided. Attendance is mandatory.

Not since his years with the Marines had he received so direct an order. He didn't know who extended the invitation, although he had his suspicions. His curiosity would soon be satisfied.

Picking up his telephone, he made several calls to clear his schedule. To his surprise, he found his schedule had already been cleared. Several appointments had been canceled, and in such a way that the most efficient use of his time was already laid out for him.

Now he was really curious.

*****

Malik entered the mosque and found a place to sit near the front. He was eagerly anticipating the talk to begin. Mujedid was sitting about ten feet in front of him. They made eye contact, and smiled a warn greeting to each other.

This mosque had a very different feel to it from the ones he used to attend. He became very comfortable from the very beginning. Not that there was much in the way of externals that were significantly different from most other mosques he's attended. The spirit of the place embraced and welcomed him as if to a long lost home.

He'd heard some very intriguing things about this mosque. Mujedid told him that most of the "regulars" that attended were musicians, singers, writers, poets, artists, scientists, philosophers, and the like. Suddenly, as the muezzin began, Malik wondered why it had taken so long for him to find this place. He drank in the atmosphere as if he'd been dying of thirst.

*****

The night of the meeting arrived. Walking out of his apartment building he saw a chauffeur standing in front of a limousine holding a placard with his name on it. Abandoning his usual caution, he stepped up to the driver. The driver's courtesy and professionalism betrayed no knowledge of what was going on. He was simply a limo driver doing his job.

During the ride, Silverstein allowed his mind to run over a number of thoughts. He had several dealings with the CIA during his military career. It could be one of the financial institutions he dealt with. Someone obviously wanted his services. This was not surprising, as he was superlatively good at what he did, and had a reputation for competence which was exceeded only by his ruthlessness. His nickname was the "Iceman"; although no one ever dared to call him that to his face. Not even his friends, of whom he had very few. He kept people at arm's length; an unusual trait for an ex-Marine.

The limousine pulled up to the appointed meeting place. A short man was standing outside waiting for him. As Silverstein approached, the man wordlessly took a computer card from his pocket, ran it through a slot on the front door, typed a security code on a keypad, and opened the door. Silverstein followed him in. They came to an elevator at the end of a dark corridor. The man pressed the button, reached inside as the door opened, placed a key in the control panel, turned it, and held the door open, gesturing for Silverstein to enter. He did and the elevator began its assent with Silverstein as the sole occupant.

As the elevator reached the penthouse Silverstein realized how relived he was that there was no music playing in it, as was the case in many office buildings. Silverstein hated all music and could not understand why anyone would listen to it. For a moment he thought of his mother, and her love for the likes of Bach, Mozart, and Handel. He was repulsed by his mother's gentleness and sincerity and hadn't spoken to her in years. He pushed the memory out of his mind.

As he stepped out of the elevator, he was greeted by a tall thin man. "Hello Mr. Silverstein. Follow me please."

Silverstein was led to a large conference room which was dominated by a large oval table with several chairs. The room was illuminated in a subdued fashion. At the head of the table was a chair with a computer monitor, a keyboard, and a trackball. Behind it was a large television screen that stood in silent dominion; waiting to assert itself. On either side of the room were ceiling to floor windows that afforded an impressive view of the city.

The tall man held out the chair at the foot of the table, saying "Please have a seat. Mr. Gorodetski will be with you momentarily." He sat down.

After a waiting period much shorter than he had expected, the door opened, and Mr. Gorodetski walked in. Tall, powerfully built, dark hair streaked with gray, steel blue eyes, a face suggestive of fourth generation Russian Jew, and wearing an expensive business suit, he stood for a second regarding his guest.

"Good evening, Mr. Silverstein" he said. "I'm pleased you could make it."

"Thank you for inviting me" Silverstein replied.

He stood and the two men shook hands. Gorodetski's powerful grip betrayed years of martial arts training. In fact, Gorodetski was an expert in Krav Maga.

Looking into his eyes, Gorodetski examined Silverstein as one sizes up an opponent; his eyes searched for weakness, assessed strategies in a predatory manner.

"Please be seated. We'll get started." He let loose his grip. Both men sat down.

"I imagine you will want to know why you have been asked here" Gorodetski began. "You have, no doubt, heard of what 'conspiracy theory' fanatics refer to as a secret society; sometimes referred to as the "Illuminati." This organization is said to exist solely for the purpose of seizing control of the world. It matters not what name it is called; in fact, strictly speaking, it has no name. For now, "Elite" will suffice. This group exists. I hold a position of considerable authority in the organization.

"Our agenda is simple: to seize control of the world. For centuries, there have been a small group of men with a unique vision. They have set in motion the machinery that will bring humanity to what has been described by some of our leaders as the "New World Order." We are now, for the first time in history, in a position where we will accomplish our goals. The whole of humanity will be united under our absolute domination as one government, one economy, one culture, one language. Once we accomplish our goal we will hold our position of absolute rule forever."

Gorodetski leaned back in his chair. "We have been aware of your abilities and accomplishments for a number of years." He typed a command into the computer and stared intently at the monitor for a few seconds. "Your education, your military record, your business, and your psychological profile have attracted and held our attention. By a special relaxation of our normal protocol, we wish to offer you membership in our Elite group."

Gorodetski leaned forward. "What are your thoughts on this?"

*****

Mujedid stood and approached the minbar. After giving the customary praises to Allah, he began.

"As you know, brothers and sisters, one of the most widely misunderstood aspects of the religion of Islam is its inherent dynamic and resiliency in the application of its principles to indigenous cultures. There is a common misconception that Islam and Western civilization are mutually incompatible and irreconcilable. I believe this to be a grave error. The reason for this is simple: Western civilization's natural progress toward its underlying purpose and potential has been subverted.

"A reporter once asked Mahatma Gandhi his opinion of Western Civilization. He said "It sounds like a good idea." The irony of his response is not lost on the perceptive mind. In essence, Western civilization does not exist.

"Many Muslims have bitter feelings towards America and Western civilization in general. While I understand their opinions and have a vaguely general agreement with many of them, and a strong disagreement with most governmental policies, I must confess a love for America (although within reasonable limits). After all, I'm an American. Much of what is interpreted as patriotism is nothing more than sentimentality for one's culture and environment. I believe it to be a natural aspect of human psychology, and I offer no apology for it.

"I say with no fear of reprisal that the application of the principals of Islam is the only hope for the survival and redemption of Western civilization; especially considering the recent advances in technology and the resulting changes in political, economic, and cultural variables.

"An objective and scientific re-examination of our civilization is desperately needed. Consider the entertainment industry; where audience's minds are systematically perverted, and performances are deliberately kept below an acceptable level of quality in order to sell enormous quantities of inferior entertainment in the form of the infantile, sensationalist, and immoral. "Consider technology and industrial development; where economic dominance and dehumanization determine how scientific knowledge is to be applied in individual and communal life - often at the expense of environmental balance.

"Consider the breakdown of families and social order; where families are subverted in an effort to establish a societal infrastructure that carries within it a built-in self-destruct mechanism. Entire populations of rootless people, ungrounded in a sense of self-worth and responsibility toward others hold positions of undeniable influence.

"Consider our political leaders whose actions may be justifiably seen as a danger to themselves and others. According to our laws, such people should be institutionalized: yet we willingly elect them to run our government, obey their every word, and turn a blind eye to the horrors and abominations they commit ever hour.

"Consider the fashion industry wherein clothing manufacturers empower ego-maniacal narcissistic homosexuals to dictate unstable sets of standards by which we are expected to determine if a human being is beautiful or not.

"Consider how the practice of religion - yes, even Islam, even us - has degenerated into either a set of meaningless rituals employed by a parasitic hierarchy, a despotic, brutal system of theocratic enslavement devoid of any trace of spirituality, mercy, or benevolence, or a toothless, docile, sugar-coated "self-help" program."

*****

So, thought Silverstein, this is it. He'd heard of the Elite. He never imagined that they would contact him, let alone offer him membership. He was intrigued by the idea.

Finally he said "What would my duties be?"

"The first item on our schedule will be a period of intense training. There are certain procedures, protocols, and bodies of information which you will need to be familiar with. After that you will begin to receive assignments from us. You will carry them out to the letter. This will continue for the rest of your life."

Gorodetski paused "Some of these assignments will be difficult. Some may be incomprehensible. The important thing is absolute obedience, and the perfect completion of your tasks. Generally you may expect your assignments to fall within your areas of expertise. However, we may from time to time call upon you to stretch your resourcefulness.

We have every confidence in you. You will also be involved in an ongoing training program. Your talents must not be wasted."

"You will be part of a team responsible for the manipulation of the world's economy in conformity with the plan we have outlined. We are presently entering the final phase of an economic program which was implemented in the middle of the 18th century. We are nearing the completion of our agenda: it will happen in our lifetime."

Gorodetski continued. "No doubt you know that all previous attempts to seize control of a nation or to initiate a political revolution have been through the use of military operations and propaganda. Our goals are similar, though we are not limited to any one nation. Our objective is the entire world. Yet our methods are very different. Our weapons are not limited to the gun or the bomb. Among our weapons are the banks, the credit system, the computers, the Internet, the educational institutions, the media, and the entertainment industry. Our methods are unlimited; and include advanced mass brainwashing, slavery, and genocide. The present stage of our program was initiated during the Eisenhower administration, and a formal declaration of war was drafted in May of 1979.

"Have you ever considered the fact that the spending habits of the cattle follow specific patterns? This is our doing. In a nutshell, we monitor the reactions, and stimulate, through a variety of means, the cattle's spending habits on areas known to have the greater, or lesser initial reactions. In the past, we had not only been able to predetermine the results, but in recent decades we have been able to manipulate them months or even years ahead of schedule. The results have been remarkably effective.

"Cattle?" asked Silverstein.

"Oh, yes" Gorodetski digressed wistfully. "We refer to the general population as 'cattle.' You've doubtless noticed that this is an accurate term. And what is the fate of cattle but steaks for our dinner tables? And why should they not be thus? Those who chose not to use their intelligence are no better than animals with no intelligence. They are cattle by choice and consent."

Silverstein smiled slightly.

*****

"I am a Muslim;" Mujedid went on "but I am also an American. I love my country and want to offer advice and guidance in the form of constructive - albeit harsh and politically unorthodox- criticism. I pray that no one will, in the course of what I anticipate will be violent disagreements, interpret a single word of my ideas as being a call to destroy America. I want the exact antithesis! I want this nation to flourish and prosper materially and spiritually. The latter is of particular importance, because there is a spiritual crisis in America that has been here since its beginnings. This is a dire spiritual crisis from which we have never recovered."

He paused thoughtfully.

"History is like human memory. It can never recapture the past. Memory attempts to reconstruct the original through an external frame of reference that inevitably falls short of its intended goal. There is an old saying that history was written by the victor. That is to say, when a power base is established, it becomes necessary to re-write history, and/or subvert scientific interpretation of historical progression and events to assist the "powers that be" in protecting their position. This is, in truth, nothing less than an admission of guilt. Here we are presented with the diametrically opposing concepts, and practices, of historical method and historical revisionism. The former describes the impartial assessment, through scientific methodology, of historical fact. The latter implies the act of rewriting history to suit the convenience of the present dialectic as is dictated by political policy.

"The rejection of the basic principles of Islam causes what may be best described as Revelation retrogression. The study of comparative religion shows that the pre-Qur'anic Revelations embody three facts. One is that each Revelation was sent to a specific nation/people at a specific point in their development. Two, they all made up a stage in the development of humanity as a whole. Three, they all pointed toward the coming of a final Revelation which would complete the Message from Allah to all of humanity. This could not have been given to humanity all at once. There had to be a period of preparation. This was especially important due to humanity's constant and almost cyclical rejection of the absolute monotheism that characterized the Revelation given to Adam and all the Prophets that followed him. This stage by stage renewal of monotheistic worship, unification of human spirituality, and elevation of human awareness and perfectibility was both restored and completed with the offering of Qur'anic Revelation. And an offering it is. There is no compulsion in Islam. The erroneous idea favored by the detractors of Islam that the Muslim is duty bound to enforce conversion to Islam is fallacious and unprovable. This being the case, the willful rejection of Islam causes a retrogression by placing humanity in a spiritual and psychological state that it had already been guided out of. The images, beliefs, and practices which embody the earlier (and in almost every instance, distorted) New Revelations are not necessary. That which may still be useful to us should not in any way contradict the basic principles of Islam.

"Yet, now we must examine where our present technological society's development is leading.

"There is a historical fact that you should know. Unlike America and Russia at the early to middle 20th century, which were industrial state-projects; the world's first technological state was Nazi Germany. In retrospect, only an idiot would deny that they were, at least in the beginning, a remarkable success. Their well-documented, atrocities aside; the fact of their ultimate defeat was due in no small part to the deviation from their original purpose of freedom from bondage to usurious interest based economics. This, by the way, was the real cause of World War Two; the banking institutions couldn't allow this to happen. But the Germans allowed them to become, by their own standards, corrupt. They indulged in the same practices, which they were attempting to rid themselves of. Ultimately, they even began collaborating with the very Zionist factions they originally declared war against. Their failure was the turning point that later allowed the technological state project to exist in subservience to usurious economics: not philosophical ideology (neither of which is desirable: Tawhid is the ultimate criteria). I am also forced to present the question of how many of the technological advances the Nazis gave the world is presently being enjoyed by us.

"As it is now, technology in subservience to usurious consumerist economics has rendered the efficient progress of both science and technology, and the development of the human spirit nearly impossible. For example; science could easily design automobile engines that are not dependent upon fossil fuel, and which do no damage to the environment. Yet this is not implemented. The reason is simple. The oil and automobile industries refuse to allow such technologies to be developed and marketed because it would mean an end to their power. The nations and corporations which rely on oil export could redesign their industries toward the manufacturer of more efficient technologies. As a result of refusal to implement this, the environment is being damaged by pollution from both automobile exhaust and oil industry accidents. an entire economy based on the extraction of a very finite natural resource stands in a state of laughable fragility, and entire populations of innocent people are butchered wholesale in wars fought over the control of this resource. There is nothing logical, efficient, or moral about the entire scenario. The same power bases could tool up for the institution of technologies to replace the idiotic domination of the internal combustion engine - a device which has been obsolete for at least three quarters of a century - thus saving their own position, and performing a valuable service to humanity. Yet they will not do this. The only explanation is that they're insane."

*****

Gorodetski continued. "Shortly after the American Revolution, an event of supreme importance to our agenda occurred, although its presence in the history books has been almost completely subdued. The very first military action following the Revolution was the Banker's War. Our esteemed forefathers took arms against the founders of the new nation. Their victory secured the grip we would eventually hold over the economy of the USA, and the world. Our next step was the elimination of metallic currency. We began this in 1871, and were able to accomplish this, on a world wide scale, in a little over a century. Some areas were less receptive to our machinations than others. Factions of Africa, Asia, the Arab world, and the Ottoman Empire were somewhat troublesome. Yet our will prevailed. Gold and silver were almost completely replaced with bank notes. These were originally redeemable for gold: now that is impossible. What the cattle once used for money, namely precious metals, is now paper: and ultimately worthless.

"As you are doubtless aware, in recent years we have begun to do away with paper notes in favor of equally worthless computer code. We also employ other terrorist actions; such as the unlimited power of the IRS. While this is being done, we apply what we call the "electronic principle."

"Electronic principle? I'm not familiar with it." Silverstein said.

"This" continued Gorodetski "is the application of the laws of electronics to monetary systems. Economic capacitance, economic resistance, economic inductance, and perhaps most important, economic amplification. Currency or deposit loans are used to induce people into surrendering their wealth in exchange for the promise of more wealth, and promissory notes instead of real compensation. Notes are loaned to individuals and governments. This created overconfidence. Then money could be made scarce, and collateral could be collected through contractual obligations. Wars are easily ignited by such means, and of course the victors could be determined by economic manipulation. World War Two had nothing to do with morality or political ideology. It was nothing more than an economic chess game. We had to neutralize Hitler's attempts to break our hold on Europe's economy. It was easy in many ways; as people like him have absolutely no egos and their psyches eventually collapse. The Gulf Wars were business transaction. So is the war in Afghanistan.

"Economic amplification is very important to us. Not many people are aware that inflation is nothing more than the printing of more paper money than can be equaled by either the gross national product. And it's amazing how people who know this ignore what it truly mean. This creates an artificial economic amplification which leads to more spending, which we control; and which leads to more spending, this in turn leads to more debt. Debt increases unchecked. And it is we to whom this debt is ultimately owed. It is not through force that we will enslave the population of the world. It is through perpetual, endless debt of money that does not exist. One of our forefathers said "Give me control over a nation's currency, and I care not who makes its laws."

*****

Mujedid took a drink of water. "Inflation is nothing more and nothing less than the printing, or creation of more paper money than can be equaled by the Gross National Product. It would then be only logical to assume that the rampant inflation that has been troubling the world's economy has been a deliberate act by the banks, and / or agencies which are responsible for the printing of paper money. Interest is a means of not only creating artificial wealth that imposes debt upon individuals, nations and industries which can never be adequately eradicated, but also makes this artificial money itself a commodity rather than a means by which real commodities may be traded. This artificial economic amplification, and the obvious destruction it imposes upon national and world economics, is essentially one of the greatest reasons why the practice of usury - interest - is forbidden in Islam: the disastrous results of this are becoming more and more obvious. We are being steered into a state of perpetual debt for astronomical amounts of money (and its interest) which does not even exist, and to an oligarchic group whom we cannot even identify. Capital originated as a symbolic representation of trade, commerce, and service. It has manifested itself as "virtual" money and debt; taking the form of an organic being: consuming, eliminating, and procreating. It is of absolute importance that anyone who uses money or is involved in any economic system whatsoever have an understanding of this.

"Usury begins when capital becomes a power unto itself. In the years immediately following the demise of communism as a world power, capitalism became, as it had already proven itself, the dominant force in world affairs. This reached an apogee due to the absence of an equal and opposite world power. The result is a worldwide monoculture of commodities and consumerism: imminent destruction of the environment, from natural resources to human imagination is inevitable. All manifestations of human mind heart and spirit are transformed into commodity. Money itself is transformed into (via the elimination of bi-metallic currency) an intangible phantom creature/force which exists outside direct human experience where it operates in its mad realm and never reaches the common man; yet dictates all aspects of social policy.

Case in point: the SWIFT web, a private banking Internet for financial institutions wherein over a trillion dollars a day are traded and circulated - but less than .0005% represents actual production of services and goods. Again, it is money existing in a "virtual" state: artificial capital which exercises control over actual money, products, services, and commodities.

"It is to usurious capitalism's good fortune that Islamic civilization is still in a state of relative dormancy. Communism and the German Nazis attempted to break the domination of capital, and failed. This was due in no small part to its major structural flaws: systematic denial of the existence of a Supreme Being through an institutionalization of "State as Object of Worship" or "State as God" via a cult of personality hero-worship of their leaders, which the Zionists have done in a very extreme way. Then there is an attempted circumventing of basic human nature. What Nietzsche called "The New Idol." Hitler clearly didn't understand Neitzsche at all."

A pause. "Additionally, it has not escaped the notice of most enlightened people that there is an ever increasing trend towards attacking Islam as a social institution, or attempting to reduce Islam to a harmless and exotic cultural ornament. Sufism has suffered a great deal from this later indignity.

"The reason for this is simple: Islam contains within its basic creed the only effective threat to the absolute domination of an oligarchic capitalist/totalitarian technocracy. Not only does Islam correctly identify usury as an evil, and diagnose its machinations, it presents an alternative system of economics that offers an asset to all an liability to none. This is the REAL reason why Islam is, quote, "The Enemy." No effective and genuine resistance against the slavery to capital can happen without

Islam.

"One element of capitalist statehood is the existence of a veiled oligarchy. In the Qur'an, Allah has told us in the Qur'an, those who consume usury are "driven mad as if by the touch of the evil one." This is actually an eloquent indication of the nature of the aforementioned oligarchy. It requires an internal denial of Al-Haqq: reality (or the incapacity to perceive or acknowledge its existence) to voluntarily work their abominations in the world. This is, I believe, one aspect of the madness Allah referred to. The oligarchy is, conceivably, even more enslaved than we are by the "beast" of capital. The elite of world finance are under the domination of the very economic system they believe they created and control.

"One would have, indeed, to suffer serious self-deception to be unaware of how this has affected humanity. It would seem that we are not aware of who truly controls commerce and industry, and the "leaders" do not lead. Their job is to divert public attention from those who hold true political power. The true significance of those who are in the public eye is not understood. The prognostications of Aldous Huxley and George Orwell have come to pass in a manner which none but a few had anticipated. Those who did anticipate it, and who attempted to explain to humanity what was happening were punished, discredited and rendered impotent. Those whose work survived are not placed in their proper historical perspective; nor are their true significance generally understood."

*****

Gorodetski took a breath, and continued. "The next important act is the control of public opinion. Our influence upon the educational institutions has been profound. We have altered the content of education to suit our needs. Our greatest innovations have been in the rewriting of history, the falsification or confusion of scientific fact, mathematics, economic studies, and the redefinition of psychological standards to seduce the public into acceptance of aimless and undisciplined behavior, drug addiction, alcoholism, and sexual deviations; especially epidemic proportions of homosexuality and pedophilia, and others in an effort to reprogram the population. They are fitting into our mold nicely. Immoralities that would have been unthinkable five years ago are now seen as fashion trends. Teenagers and young adults follow this with amazing obedience for no reason other than that they are told to do so by the television and magazines. We even manipulate their speech patterns by these means. Watch a "prime time sitcom", and then examine the vernacular of the cattle over a period of time. You will notice unmistakable parallels.

"In education, the important thing to remember is that the cattle that come to school at age five possess some kind of allegiance to parents, to religion, to a nation, etc. They are to be treated not as students, but as patients. They are sick and must be cured or punished. Has it escaped your notice that the architectural design of elementary and high schools bear more than a passing resemblance to that of a prison?

"Military control of the cattle is also an option we exercise as is needed. One way that this is done is through the police. Doubtless you've noticed that the police forces have been given, shall we say, a wide breadth of discretion in certain matters? Gun control is another way in which we exercise control of the masses. They are whipped into a frenzy of fear by the news and entertainment media, while we cultivate the baser factions of the criminal element, and terrorist groups. Osama Bin Laden, the Taliban, Al- Qaeda, Sadaam Hussain, and the like are rabid dogs that we bred and armed. Our original intentions were to gain control of the oil resources of Afghanistan, and to subdue any potential threat from unstable elements in the USSR or China. We let them loose upon the world to do whatever damage they liked. They thought they were helping the "cause" of Islam, when in reality; they are very far from their religion in all but superficiality. Some can't even practice the basics of their religion correctly. Needless to say, our own people hold positions of leadership in these groups. As a result, the cattle are practically begging us to take from them an otherwise effective means of self-defense. In the end the only ones who are armed are criminals, terrorists, or the police and militia. All of whom operate under our command.

"In fact, the police and armed forces are also subject to our brainwashing technology; in order to instigate their bloodlust. They responded amazingly well to this. Just like attack dogs. Their limited intelligence is an asset to us. This system was actually designed by the German Nazis and rehearsed during their brief reign.

"Another way in which we are accomplishing this is through the modification of Martial Law. In the late 1960's the wording of the criteria regarding the invocation of Martial Law was changed from "War, threat of war, or imminent attack" to "Any conceivable national emergency." This allows us a wide range of interpretation; and, of course, we dictate the paradigms of that interpretation. Our exacerbation of inner city crime, the drug trade, domestic terrorism, and the Middle East and Balkans conflicts and the like have allowed us to inflame public fear of all manner of anarchy and chaos; real or imagined. We may then suspend the Constitution and impose Martial Law. The cattle will not argue. Similarly, few are aware that there exists no governmental procedure for the repeal of Martial Law. The same goes for national security alerts.

"We have a number of projects lined up; NAFTA, the NAU, and others"

*****

"The practice of science in Western civilization has allowed a serious error to become the foundation upon which it is built" Mujedic went on "namely, the concept that events and actions within an experiment or process can be isolated and compartmentalized from the event of the entire universe. Science is assumed to work solely upon the interaction of mass vs. energy. One of the motivating factors involved is the economic factor: the proliferation of consumerist profits being the sole basis upon which science is understood and developed. This is wrong. It is ultimately suicidal.

"There is also the blinding intoxication that accompanies technology. Now, this is not to say that Muslims are forbidden the use and development of technology and science. Quite the antithesis! What is to be considered is the fact that technology is not a passive instrument that has no effects upon the society of man. Technology is like a wild animal that must be trained and mastered; or it will master us. We see evidence of this all around us. Something that is not widely known that you should be aware of concerns Satanism. Many of you will know it as devil worship; and there is some truth in this. However, Satanism's deeper meanings constitute the worship of not only the flesh, sensuality, and materialism, but also the worship of science and technology. The human being is exalted through the development of technology. Through the submission not to Allah, but to a technological process, man's technological creation becomes his master: a demented, out-of-control Frankenstein's monster created in the image of the human ego.

"The worst part of technology is that it gives no indication that the human being must develop his or her self, first and foremost, or the power inherent in technological progress will mirror their own spiritual bankruptcy and cause a disaster.

"It must be understood that the whole of Allah's creation is a singularity which manifests itself as a multiplicity. This multiplicity is inextricably linked with itself. This is exemplified in the phenomenon that is the basis of the only complete science: the study of waveforms. All things exist as waveforms, all things therefore, are one. The understanding of this will enable the Muslim to understand the inner nature of his and her position as custodians of creation.

"This understanding extends to all things; including business and economics. The manner in which we as Muslims conduct our business and economic affairs is clearly described in Qur'an and Hadith. The importance of adhering to these principles is clearer now than in any point in history. The condition of world economics has gotten to the point where if we do not develop and administer an alternate system of economy based on Islamic principles, we will be faced with absolute economic and societal ruin. Since the 1700's, the banking system has increasingly employed the use of usury (rib'a) based economics to create artificial wealth; i.e. wealth that does not exist anywhere except on paper, or as computer information.

"In recent times, those few Communist nations who are holding on to their ideals have been forced into drastic modifications of their internal and international policies: mostly in the area of economics. Communism never worked economically. It cannot. It has a basic structural flaw that sets itself against the natural human desire of acquisition of wealth. Quality workmanship is nullified by the removal of profit incentive. Like it's opposite, capitalism, it is obsolete.

"What few people dare think about is that there is a third alternative. This arises from the desperate need to eliminate and transcend the bicameral assembly.

"Modern economists and industrialists, and subsequently, the scientists in their employ, perceive the material world not only as the whole of existence, but allow a tunnel vision to develop; i.e. nothing exists, or has any relevance, beyond their area of expertise and source of capital. If an economic or industrial project were to cause damage to the world as a whole, these consequences would be ignored. They are masters of the "take the money and run" attitude, necessitating an Orwellian Doublethink process of world view. Islamic economics and science cannot function like this. Its very existence is utterly dependent upon the perception of all systems being interconnected, all action having universal repercussions (including the effect upon the unseen, and the ultimate condition of the human soul), and the inescapable acknowledgment of the existence and direct influence of Allah. When monetary, governmental or scientific institutions deviate from this, in essence deviating from La Illaha Ilallah ("There is no god but Allah") then the structure of the system begins to collapse.

The manifestations of Western culture, i.e. computers, mass media, etc are inextricably woven into the fabric of human life. We are faced with two possible scenarios when assessing their compatibility or incompatibility with an American Islamic culture. One is that they be altered to suit the needs and essence of the next phase of Islamic civilization. The other is their complete elimination. It should be kept in mind, however, that the later cannot occur without a cataclysmic and catastrophic destruction of the host society. The indisputable and inevitable truth of this observation makes our choice in the matter clear especially in light of the aftermath of the events on September 11th 2001."

*****

Gorodetski paused thoughtfully, and continued.

"It is vitally important that you understand that the cattle are unfit to rule their own lives. Nietzsche had an idealistic prognostication about the rise of a race of "Overmen": a humanity that would have no need for laws or morality. In some ways he was wrong. Yet the need for such is of paramount importance. It was up to us to become that Overman ourselves. Left to the devices of the cattle, the human race would not have survived this century. I don't need to explain why. You can see the truth for yourself. Their extinction would have insured the end of our power: an unacceptable prospect. The cattle owe us their lives: and we are intent upon collecting this debt with interest."

"Let me ask you something" Silverstein interjected. "I understand what you are describing. I recognize it and admire your resourcefulness and ingenuity. The problem is stopping others from perceiving it. How is this accomplished?"

"Really, Silverstein." Gorodetski said, with amused disgust. "That shows an astonishing lack of imagination on your part. Remember; we control the media. We present them with any piece of information we wish. We insert whatever insane idea we wish into their heads. We remove it at will, and replace it with anything of our choosing. We even manipulate the method of linguistic communication; making ideas which contradict our dialectic unintelligible and incomprehensible.

"So what if someone figures out part of what we do? What can he do? He has no way of proving what he "sees." Nor can he take effective action against us. Communication of his ideas is impossible. Those who manage to make enough noise to attract attention almost invariably attract the emotionally unstable. These continue to extrapolate ideas of their own which may have their genesis in reality, but deviate to serve only their own egomania. Some years ago, a Navy Intelligence officer violated Elite secrets by writing a book about what we've been doing. Do you know what we did? We put his book in the "New Age" section of the bookstores. This effectively discredited him, although we eliminated him later. Doubtless you have seen "rebels", "alternative" groups such as White Supremacists, Black Nationalists, New Age cults, "pop" subcultures, UFO enthusiasts, conspiracy theorists, Millennium nuts, etc., etc. We have cultivated all these. We cultivate racism in specific groups. Have you ever read the Emancipation Proclamation? There is nothing in it that truly abolishes slavery. The exploitable loopholes are obvious to any first year law student. Yet the cattle are told the exact antithesis. This is what they believe because they lack the courage and the ambition to investigate these things for themselves and think clearly. They are too busy with their petty amusements.

"Diversion is the important thing, Silverstein. We divert the public's attention from reality, and keep them busy arguing over meaningless controversies. We overload them with information impossible to assimilate. We make it impossible to distinguish truth from lies. Every now and again, we create some kind of disaster, war, or other calamity. With every calamity, the cattle become more and more frightened, and beg us to remove their liberties in exchange for peace. They say "Leave me alone." So we build prisons with invisible bars and guards they can't see or identify that they practically walk into without coercion. We keep them occupied by amusements and occasional distress. We erode their freedoms and they argue about Janet Jackson exposing herself at a football game or whether Brad Pitt and Anjelina Jolie are going to break up. Every one of the cattle looks at the world around them, sees in some vague way that things are getting worse, and says 'Something must be done.' Nothing ever gets done. Their plight gets worse, and they continue to argue themselves into frenzy about insignificant nonsense, and render themselves more and more impotent. Thus, we are rendered more and more omnipotent."

*****

Mujedid paused. "It must be remembered that any human manipulation of the world in which we live has universal repercussions. It is suicidal to believe that the principle of Oneness is optional when we make a decision in this matter. The whole of creation is one. Allah is One. Human beings are the only creatures that cannot survive unless we change our environment. There is almost no limit to the secrets we can unlock, almost no limit to the things we may achieve. Yet this is not a license to attempt to remake Allah's creation in the image of our own vanities. To do so would be to labor under the lie that we created the universe; or can re-create it to suit our vain liking. Scientists, entrepreneurs, etc. must fight a great Jihad to keep from making false gods out of their abilities and goals. This form of idolatry, when applied to science, industry, economics, etc. is the most self-destructive act a community can perform. Nothing will destroy an individual or a nation with more efficiency than the rejection of the basic truth of "La Ilaha Ilallah."

"We are living in a Dark Age.

"As bleak as this scenario appears, all is not lost to us. Islam is the only religion which encompasses all aspects of life. It offers a complete way of life and method of thought. It unites the community and insures individual freedom. Human rights are guaranteed by Divine Order; not by human bestowal. It is the only religion whose history proves: from the model communities of Mecca and Medina, to the Abbasids, the Moors, the Ottomans, to the fledgling Islamic communities in Europe and America, it's claim of being, in it's pure form, free from human error. The Islamic method of economics offers the opportunity for everyone to acquire wealth without causing harm to one's soul or to the structure of the community. Islamic economics is efficient and holistic. It works on scientific and spiritual, not political terms. It does not allow the proliferation of parasitic business and economic practices; while allowing the acquisition of wealth. There exists in modern society an entire category of professions that are based on unreal values, and contribute nothing to the economic structure of society. The entire apparatus of making money only through the manipulation of money is wasteful, corrupting, parasitic, and ultimately distorts the true value of money, goods, resources, and services. This cannot exist in a truly

Islamic society.

"This is good news for humanity. All of humanity has everything to gain by embracing the Islamic methodology and belief system. We also stand to lose everything by its rejection."

*****

"Before I forget," Gorodetski said, "Here is a book you need to read. The author is one of the great men of our Elite. He outlines an era that involves the gradual appearance of a more controlled society dominated by an elite, unrestrained by traditional values."

Opening it, he read, *"Already, the social elites of the more advanced countries are globalist in spirit and outlook. The nation-state is yielding its sovereignty"*

There was a moment of silence.

"Do you believe in God, Silverstein?" Gorodetski asked abruptly.

"No" said Silverstein, bluntly and with finality.

"We are God" Gorodetski said, with quiet intensity. "Remember that. There is no God but the Elite. We control thought; we control world events; we control lives. He who controls thought controls reality. Reality only exists through human consciousness and human imagination. This is a key factor to our power. Every despot, every tyrant, every dictator knew this. Yet our predecessors such as the Nazis and Communists have proven themselves to be weaklings. They failed to take the reality control principle to its natural end. We will not make this mistake. We are the absolute masters of this principle; therefore we are the absolute masters of the world. We are God."

Silverstein sat spellbound. His mind reeled with what can only described as the intoxication of power.

Gorodetski saw it in his eyes and smiled. "Makes your head spin, doesn't it? Wait: this is just the beginning. There are other ongoing projects we are at work upon. These include mass psycho cybernetic mind control, outer space colonization, our extraterrestrial programs, and our plans for de-populating the Earth. You will be informed of the details of these in time."

Gorodetski smiled again: an unnerving sight.

"By the way, accounts in several banks have been placed at your disposal. You will need great resources to accomplish your tasks. They are yours to do with as you wish. No one will question your use of this money. The IRS is no longer your concern: they are for the cattle, not you."

"I'm grateful" Silverstein said, not without sincerity. "I have one question. Will we expect effective resistance from anyone?"

Gorodetski became silent for a moment. A look flickered across his face for a second, like a cornered animal.

"Some religious groups" he said slowly, as if in anger "have caused us concern. We are somewhat taken aback at the recent rise in conversions to the religion of Islam, despite several centuries of effort to prevent it. One of our greatest accomplishments had been the abolition of the Caliphate in the former Ottoman Empire after World War One; and the manipulation of the Middle East's oil based economy. Yet they seem to have resisted our efforts, and are regrouping. They, some sects of Protestant Christians, and a small handful of others not only clearly perceive our work, but have, unlike the rest of the cattle, absolutely no fear of us. We are watching them and will determine what action will be necessary to neutralize any potential threat from them."

Gorodetski took a breath. "I believe that will be all for now." He stood. "We will be in touch soon. A man named Brown will contact you."

Silverstein stood and approached Gorodetski. Before they shook hands, Gorodetski stared into his eyes. "There is one thing I advise you keep in mind. Betray us, disobey us, or even fall below an acceptable level of competence, and you will know our wrath. You will find that your body's incapacity for feeling sufficient pain to pay for your crimes will not deter us from exacting our revenge. You will not find us merciful or forgiving. We know everything about you. We are always watching you."

Silverstein, though not easily scared, had no doubt that his comments were to be taken literally. Gorodetski held out his hand, smiled and said "Welcome aboard." They shook hands.

"My assistant will show you out. Farewell Mr. Silverstein" The tall thin man had materialized, and was holding the door open for him.

During the ride home, Silverstein pondered his new found success. This was the greatest moment of his life. He would finally achieve the great things he'd always deemed of. Power beyond imagining. Yet something bothered him. Something was wrong.

Something.

He pushed the thought out of his mind.

*****

Mujedid continued. "One of the greatest errors that bureaucratic governments make in dealing with their charges is the restriction of research and intellectual pursuits. Power bases will invariably suppress research that does not conform to its immediate needs. The unlimited quest for knowledge will produce, in the society ruled by an inept government, unwanted competition, and a host of innovative products and ideas that are not easily captured by their inside investors. Furthermore, innovation in research in the sciences and arts will always produce results that are better than the established bureaucratic procedures: and bureaucracies desperately wish to avoid being made to look inept! Like all forms of tyranny, this is an act of suicidal inability to embody a dynamic and resiliency that will grow with the natural need of humans to expand their boundaries.

"And it must be done. The universe is full of infinite variables that cannot conform to a regimented confinement of investigation. I ask the reader if he/she is aware that Allah's creation is a wondrous thing! Atoms are not particles or waveforms; but both. Put aside your fixed, preconceived notions. Allah's Handiwork cannot be understood by narrow and inflexible perceptions. You have only one awareness; a dynamic awe before the infinite!

"And what about forgiveness? The root word of astaghfirullah is `ghafara,' which carries the same meaning of the Arabic root `satara,' meaning: `to cover over.' Therefore, the meaning of the phrase Astaghfirullah is: 'I seek the covering of Allah's Attributes.' No human being is free from a desperate need of this.

"My general focus has been on Western/ Euro-American thought and philosophy should be seen only as a means to a much greater end. It is of supreme importance that the various nations, philosophies, schools of thought, cultural variables, etc. be seen as interdependent components of a greater whole. The unifying factor here is Tawhid.

"While every nation, race, culture, etc, exists and has its own essential characteristics and nature, the mindset of nationalism must be avoided. This is not to say that a reasonable love of one's people is irrational or psychopathic - as some variations of modern "political correctness" would have us believe. Indeed, the Prophet (sas) once said as much. But when it degenerates into nationalism, then nothing but madness and degeneration may be expected. The Prophet Muhammad (sas) described nationalism as a malignant disease. The analogy is rather accurate: a cancerous growth within the body - the community, and collective mindset and spirit - which either serves no useful purpose, or threatens to contaminate and ultimately destroy the entire organism.

"It is necessary to work towards the building of a healthy community worldwide where the conditions which produce oppression, poverty, immorality, crime and ecological destruction are impossible. I advise you to keep in mind that the greatest opposition to this will come from those who have the greatest control over the world's economy (although they will probably employ, through cowardice, the use of mercenaries to protect themselves). These are the real enemies to contend with; and they will not be easy to find. The perception of the nature and implementation of the weapons being used against us, and the methods of distracting us from this situation, are designed to prevent us from perceiving the fact that we are being attacked. We are unaware of our own slavery.

"We must resist the urge to generalize the potential identity of these enemies: to point at a group of people and say "it's their fault!" These prejudicial oversimplifications will render us impotent and ridiculous: and those who hate us will laugh with delight at the fact that we have destroyed ourselves with little effort on their part. Instructions on the successful engagement of these difficulties and how our goals of the creation of a truly Islamic society may be accomplished will be found in the Qur'an and the teachings of the Prophet Muhammad (sas).

"And our struggle in this area must never end. We will never arrive at 'It.' Never. There will always be a new difficulty to overcome, a new level of spiritual awareness and being to achieve, a new veil to penetrate. This is infinite. We will never arrive at a stage where we will be justified in saying "This is it."

"Here, I must ask us to meditate on our own shortcomings - and make no mistake: I include myself in this admonishment! A new paradigm does not take effect by 'convincing' an old paradigm to conform to its tenants. It does so only when the old paradigm dies. Old paradigms die only when they are no longer relevant to their surroundings, or when the proponents of the new paradigm cause its termination. The Ummat cannot bring into existence a paradigm or system of Islamic civilization (in whatever manifestation it may be) unless it believes in its absolute correctness. To illustrate: those economists with superior vision understand that the only thing that will prevent the inevitable implosion of the current usury based economic system dominating the world would be the institution of a non-interest based system of bi-metallic currency and barter system. The Ummat are the only people whose very moral and psychological foundation in Qur'anic Revelation allows them the capability of instituting it. Yet it will never happen unless the Ummat accepts this inevitable truth.

"Nor should the financial institutions see this as a threat. It is, in fact, their only means of survival. They are trapped in an economic cul-de-sac that will inevitably implode unless action is taken to avert the danger. Islam offers a practical means by which this is accomplished.

"We often fail, through ignorance, impatience, and even arrogance, to effectively present Islam to the non-Muslim in terms which he / she understands. Some brothers and sisters refuse to speak to non-Muslims at all. Our poor daw'a strategies are evident in our speech, deeds, and our arts; which are often how we are perceived. Many times I am asked about Islam. Almost always I am told that they "didn't know" about the things I tell them, and this in situations where they are often in the company of Muslims. While this is not always the case, it happens all too often. Only Allah makes Muslims, but we are the instruments through which He works His Will. Sadly these instruments are often not always well suited to their task. This can be remedied in a variety of ways.

"Herein is illustrated a great part of the responsibility of the Muslim: the creation and presentation of a Beautiful Example which inspires the heart, mind and spirit of the listener to seek Allah. If the non-Muslim can not perceive the true message we carry, it is not our fault;

Allah told us in the Qur'an that there are some upon whose hearts are a seal, and if Allah does not guide them then we can't either. The exposure to Islam will not make much of a difference: yet we are not in a position to always accurately perceive who will accept Islam, and when - which is another failing on our part. Some of us give daw'a and expect all within earshot of us to immediately run to the mosque and take shahadah. It doesn't work that way. In fact it may be years before the message we carry takes hold; and we may never bear witness to the fruits of our labor. Sadly we want our impatience to be satisfied immediately and often so we can point to the new Muslim and say "Look what I did."

"The Muslim must never, for one second, lose sight of the fact that he is Allah's instrument. Allah made clear in the Qur'an that humanity is His vicegerents on earth, and that the Believers are the khalifah - leaders - of humanity. If we understood what is meant by the fact that we are expected to behave as leaders among Allah's ambassadors of Divinity, we would live very different lives. We would understand that our main Jihad is within our own hearts. The Prophet (sas) described two Jihads: the Jihad al-Ahsar, which is the struggle to protect one's community or accomplish some goal; and the Jihad al-Akbar, which is the struggle with the evil that exists in our own souls.

"Organized religion, especially Islam, must be constantly on guard with its motives behind their method of Scriptural and Prophetic interpretation. Why is religion established? Why are religious bodies so passionately concerned with survival? To what end? What good is survival if you do not survive whole: including spiritually? Is a power base worth meeting your end in a dogmatic self-idolatry? Leaders: ask yourself if you can truly see the difference between hubris and Revelation!

"The fool puts great effort into finding fault in others. The wise man seeks out the faults within him. I have tried to do both. I am not without my faults. I, being the humblest of Allah's servants, have no real power in this world. My voice is very small and still compared to the resounding shout of others. I have no authority to call for Jihad or to issue fatwas; and frankly, I wouldn't want it if it were available to me. But if I did, I'd call upon all of humanity to the Jihad al-Akbar!

And make no mistake; it is a Jihad. I ask you as I ask myself something. Is our religion real if it carries no risks and costs us nothing? Is our religion real if we become fat and complacent in it? Is it real if we commit atrocities, or permit others to commit atrocities in its name and let our hands fall into our laps and say "Masha Allah"? What have we permitted ourselves to degenerate into? Are we guilty of the same debauchery, fraud, and mindlessness of religious conventionality that we say we despise in others?

"All temples, shrines and prayer houses, synagogues, churches and mosques; whether imposing pinnacles of architecture, or run-down shacks, are merely spiritual dojos. Prayers, rituals, ceremonies and observances are exercises to open the perception the believers in awe of the presence and power of Allah. But no matter what the denomination, truth/god/self/void is one and all pervading, knowing all the innermost secrets and intents from without and from within. In timeless, ever-present reality the prayer starts when the believer leaves the temple.

"Things like the Shari'ah and Ijtihad are a means to an end. The root of the word Shari'ah is a verb meaning to enter a body of water and drink from it. This presents a very different idea than the idea of 'Law.'

Perhaps another facet is that the Shari'ah are like the ropes that held Odysseus to the mast of his ship, so he could hear the song of the Sirens; and the wax in his shipmate's ears so they wouldn't be destroyed by that same song.

"In Qur'an, 6:32, Allah asked: '*What is the life of this world but play and amusement? But best is the home in the hereafter, for those who are righteous. Will ye not then understand?*'

"Our answer, the only honest answer we can give: 'No Allah, we do not understand!'

"If we had within us a trace of real taqwa, those questions would terrify us like nothing short of the Day of Judgment could. Because one day, Allah will put us face to face the lies we told ourselves, and believed.

"But there is still time to chose the straight path. May Allah guide us to success in this life and the Hereafter."

He then closed the sermon, and called for the iqamah to announce that the prayer is about to begin.

Malik was looking around. His friend Tarik never showed up for jumma. This was very unlike him. Too bad; he wanted him to meet Mujedid.

*****

Tarik sat in the room where they had locked him. There was a mirror embedded in the wall (who were they kidding?) and no mirror. There was nothing more than a table, and two chairs.

He had been here for a couple of hours. Earlier that day he had been walking down the street when a black van pulled up beside him. Four men in black suits jumped out and quickly pulled him into the van. One of them told him that if he cooperated, he may live to see tomorrow. He decided to give the impression of cooperation.

He knew what they wanted. Only days before, when he was on the Internet, he had come across a forbidden website that existed on a private internet network. Tarik was very good with computers; but this must have been some kind of fluke; an accident. Unable to resist, he downloaded files from the website, and read them.

He was taken aback at what he read. It seems that a group of astrophysicists have determined that the space-time continuum will collapse. It was beyond their capabilities to determine exactly when this will happen; but it was inevitable and unstoppable. Colonization of outer space would not be sufficient to escape the catastrophe.

The entire universe was collapsing. Humanity was doomed. No other conclusion to come to.

But there was something else these people believed they could do. Tarik was horrified at what they were seriously contemplating,,,,,

Tarik knew that this was something big. He also knew that public knowledge of this find would cause widespread panic throughout the world.

If anyone believed it.

Just then the door opened. Two men walked in. They were wearing black suits, black shoes and socks, white shirts, black ties, dark sunglasses, and the ridiculous haircuts one normally associates with government agents or politicians. One of them sat down. The other stood behind Tarik.

The man who sat opposite him pulled a pack of cigarettes from his pocket, and wordlessly offered one to Tarik. He refused. The cigarettes went back into the pocket.

"My name is Morris Silverstein" the man began. "I belong to a branch of an Intelligence agency that the public knows nothing about. I will not waste time: you are here because of the website you accessed. We want to know how you did it, and why."

Tarik told him how he did it; down to the last detail. He had nothing to hide. It was, after all, an accident. Tarik, a humble man by nature, had no interest in being a "spy" or anything equally dramatic. The interrogation was, so far, not as bad as Tarik had expected. Silverstein, while not friendly, was at least fair, reasonable, and rational. Something one doesn't expect from government or intelligence agents.

"You realize" Silverstein said, after Tarik answered all his technical questions "That the information you have is highly classified. This was a very serious security breach, accidental or otherwise. Only a handful of people in the world are aware of what you now know. It is important that we do not allow this information to reach the public."

Tarik began to laugh.

"Silverstein's eyes narrowed at him, visible even behind the dark glasses. "What's so funny?"

"What's funny is the irony of the whole situation," Rachid said. The two men looked at each other. Rachid said, "You don't get it, do you?"

"No. Spell it out for me." Silverstein said icily.

"I don't suppose that it has escaped your notice that I'm a Muslim."

"And this means what?"

"Do you realize that we have known about this for centuries? Since the Qur'an was revealed to the Prophet, peace be upon him, this has been common knowledge to us. Obviously our ancestors had no knowledge of black holes and the like, and we didn't know the details; but the general idea has been with us for a long time. There are many references to the Day of Judgment in the Qur'an. One of them describes the sky rolling up like a scroll. Others describe the sky being rent in twain. I could go on. The point I'm making here is that to any Believer, this information comes as no surprise. Our Scriptures have been telling us that it would happen. We've been waiting for it and preparing for it. I wasn't surprised at all."

Absolutely nonplussed, and hiding it well, Silverstein said "You knew about this because of the scriptures of your religion?"

"Yes. The thing that you are so worried about, apart from the fear of uncontrollable public panic, is what will happen after the Great Event. We know, in general, what will happen. We have been instructed on how to prepare for it, and we have been sharing this instruction and inviting you to join us since the 7th century! I'm not worried. I believe, and bear witness, that there is no god except Allah, and that Muhammad is His servant and messenger!"

With that, Silverstein stood up, nodded to his companion. The companion pulled a gun from his belt and shot Tarik twice in his head.

As Tarik fell to the ground, Silverstein turned to look at him. He was shocked to see a smile and a look of absolute peace and contentment on his face; his right hand in a loose fist with the index finger extended.

Silverstein walked out.

That look would haunt him the rest of his life.

*****

Two years later, during Ramadan, Silverstein was killed when a drunken driver smashed into his car. The drunk was arrested, sentenced to four years, and converted to Christianity in prison. Upon his release, he became a respected pastor of a church and a frequent attendee at Alcoholics Anonymous meetings.

He often expressed remorse for having killed an innocent man.

When Gorodetski learned of Silverstein's death, he mourned for a moment. He truly liked Silverstein, and had high hopes for him.

That night, he looked out his office window, and said to himself, "He'll be back."

Ancient Sunlight

There's a storm outside

The elements rage blue and white

Furious wind stings flesh and non-flesh alike with cold effect

Small lights and grottoes lonely in this maelstrom.

My winged horses fly around jagged cliffs that descend into howling
waters and ascend toward a raging moon,

Against which winds vindictively smash themselves.

My flames burn like a twin serpent that ascends in spiraling columns of
light;

I struggle to master this power.

My darkness houses a world of forms and furious energies that seek
balance at any cost.

If Allah's mighty power is displayed in the violence of the storm, in the
uprooting of the trees, in the smashing of the buildings, and in the
making of the mountains light as leaves carried by water;

If all this could not awaken you, how could I succeed?

I suppose a light kiss on the cheek may have done the trick.

But you are still frightened of the storm, aren't you?

We all are; and for good reason.

That storm was waiting for us since the beginning of time.

And while the sky fell, we argued about minutiae and irrelevancies

Ancient sunlight waits like diamonds and pearls,

Ancient sunlight threatens to expose our follies;

Ancient sunlight offers to shine a path through our self imposed darkness.

The storm has not let up, it rages on,

Heedless of our human fragility.

But it will return to its state of equilibrium.

In the meantime,

If I forgot myself in the majesty, it is because myself and the majesty became one

Indeed, they always were,,,

But I forgot!

Bedtime Story for Musicians

Once upon a time, in a faraway kingdom of musicians, there lived an evil sorcerer. Nobody liked him, and he didn't like anybody else. He just lived in a rundown castle, casting spells and talking to psychotic djinns.

One day, he decided to do something very bad. He went into the deepest, darkest part of the forest, cut down a tree, and made a musical instrument out of it. The instrument had 19 strings, and was very difficult to play and tune. So much so, that, after he sent it to the king, nobody in the whole kingdom could play a single note on it. All it would do is make terrible noises that made people sick and unhappy when they listened to it. The musicians from the kingdom tried their best to make it sound nice, but they just couldn't. After years of trying, finally, the king took the terrible instrument, and locked it away.

After more years had passed, news came to the kingdom of a master musician from a faraway land that was traveling, and was going to visit the kingdom. The people were very happy; because they always liked it when new music would come to them. The master musician came to the kingdom, and the king sent a messenger to invite him to stay at the castle. The master musician was happy to accept the king's generous offer.

The king and the master musician were eating and drinking together, and the master musician asked him something. He wanted to know if it was true that there was an instrument nobody could play. The king said "Yes. I have it locked away. It's something an evil sorcerer made; and it is terrible! Its music makes people sick, and nobody can play it." The master musician asked if he could try to play it. The king was hesitant; he didn't want people to suffer anymore. But the master musician persuaded him to let him try.

That evening, after news of the master musician's request had spread, a group of brave people attended a recital where the master musician would try to play the evil instrument. They were a little worried; would they get sick like the others? Would the instrument make terrible sounds? The master musician sat in a chair and the instrument was brought to him. Nobody had touched or tuned it in a long time, or even cleaned it. The master blew the dust off it, rubbed some of the dirt from it, took a breath, and played a note.

To everybody's surprise, a beautiful sound came from the instrument! The master musician caressed the instrument, like someone petting and soothing a wild animal. Then, the instrument remembered that it was made from a piece of wood, and it started to sing all the songs of the trees, forest, rain, rivers, birds, and animals. With every melody the master musician played, it reminded the instrument of its origins; and it created the seasons, phases, and essence of nature with every note that came from it. The beauty of the forest was there, in the room of the castle, and the people were enraptured.

After the performance, the king and all the people approached the master musician and asked him how he did it. He said "The musicians before me failed because they only tried playing their own songs on the instrument. They were vain, and never saw past themselves. As for me, I let the music play itself. There was no 'I'. Did the instrument become me, or did I become the instrument? Even I don't know - and it doesn't matter; all that matters is the music."

After that, the king invited the master musician to stay in his kingdom. The master musician accepted his offer, and all the musicians from far and wide came to him to learn. Soon the world was filled with master musicians, and all ears were filled with the beautiful music they made.

And as for the evil sorcerer, one day he disguised himself as an old man, and went to hear the master musician play the instrument he'd made. He was so overcome with the music that he renounced his evil ways, and became one of the most well liked people in the kingdom.

A Dangerous Love Letter to Allah.

I remembered you when my enemy's knife tried to bath itself in my blood. I wished to kiss the weapon; the shining blade reminded me of the light from your eyes.

You veil yourself from me, yet your beauty is condensed through what little you show. Gold and diamonds are buried deep in the earth, pearls wait at the bottom of the ocean. The roses of the Sultan's garden are safe behind fortress walls. The unworthy may not hold them.

Yet what glimpses and evidence we see inspires us to boldness, and daring us to sit upon a king's throne. Beauty insinuates itself within You. Bathed in a moment of peace; evidence a Great Promise. If only the tears of the rose could wash away the pains and trials of the world,,,

But it is enough, always enough.

The cup is raised. Scent of Wine overshadows the chains of the world.
I drink liquid rubies of light, red hyacinthine lips mirrored upon the stained glass of this Cup. One drop, and my thirst is quenched forever. One drink, and the whole universe and everything in it can never again satisfy my needs.

Oh Allah! You made me, and You wounded me! Am I condemned to wait, suffocating in this desert of shadows? Am I doomed to wander the wastes crying the Name of my Lover, while the light of pitiless stars insults my pain? My sadness and longing proves that the rose can be pricked by its own thorn.

O Allah! Who are You? Is this silence a gift more merciful than truth?

A True Story.

"BEEPBEEPBEEPBEEPBEEP!

Unh!

BEEPBEEPBEEPBEEPBEEP!

"Yeah! Yeah! I'm up! Gimme a minute!"

What a way to start the day; negotiating with an alarm clock. I'm not a morning person. I'm accustomed to the night.

This week, however, they have me on the morning shift.

After putting on a pot of coffee and feeding the cat, I made wudu and lay out my prayer rug. Sometimes it's an effort to concentrate on Allah. Other thoughts of events, plans schedules compete for my attention. I do my best.

A moment of peace comes to me: seemingly a reward for the effort of my internal struggle.

After a cup or three of coffee, a shower, and dressing, I head out the door.

It's a hot morning: almost 80 degrees at 5:45am. The air is like soup. Summer in New York City. People are up and about. Workers in the food industry are already busy at their tasks. Trucks are loaded and unloaded. Their labors have not yet completely shattered the stillness cf the night: neither has the sun which is slowly illuminating the world.

Homeless people are out going about their business: interacting with each other in the mysterious intricacies of their rejected subculture. Their almost predatory skills at panhandling are not diminished by the early hour. They either got an early start, or are basking in the afterburner of the previous night.

People are on their way to work. Some dressed in suits; others in casual attire. Like ants they pour into the train station. I pour with them. I regard them with pity. They look like zombies. All day long they go about their horrible existence.

I look at my watch. I'm a good 45 minutes early! On an impulse I jump out of the train a couple stops too soon. Today, I take the long way to work.

The momentum of the day is beginning to pick up. Despite this, I am safe within the fortress of my daydreams. I allow myself the luxury of flights of fancy: imagination unleashed. I have a world to myself. I also admire the peculiar beauty of the city at this hour. The indefinable vibe. The calm before the storm.

People all around me are either working or on their way to work. One man is in a small shop devoted to glassworks. He's obviously the master of his own domain. The rest? Slaves to corporations. Robots. Pavlov's dogs scurrying to and fro: unaware of their own misery. How fortunate I am to be immune to this poison. I can see them now: going about their tasks mechanically. Predictable units functioning with drone-like efficiency. Eyes as dead as burned out fuses in a fusebox.

Instructions and decrees issued from "The Management": an indefinable and inflexible hierarchy which is never questioned. Pavlov is ringing his bell.

85

I arrive at work about ten minutes early. I greet the guy I'm relieving, and he briefs me on the events of the shift, and what I'll need to know. After the formalities, I sit and have coffee. We make small talk as he gets ready to leave. Just then the "hotline" phone rings: the phone reserved for the exclusive use of my boss. I stop talking in mid- sentence, mid-word; and jump up to answer the phone before it could ring a second time.

Pavlov's dogs, indeed.

Requiem for a Swamp

I grew up in Southeast Wisconsin. There was a large field about a mile and a half from the house where I grew up. It had, at the northeast side of the field, a swamp. We used to go and play in the swamp. It was not very big, probably smaller thanwe thought it was. But it was ours. Not literally: we owned nothing. But we considered it ours.

The entire field and swamp were our sanctuary. We would meet there, play there, fight with each other, and interact in our little subculture. We build forts there, made fires. They never caused damage: we knew how to handle fire. As we grew older, we would smoke cigarettes and marijuana, and occasionally explored the strange and forbidden territory of the opposite sex.

In the spring, the colors were vibrant, the good earth waking from her slumber. It brought promise of new life. In the summer the air was hot and humid; but clean. The breezes and sunlight seemed to infuse us with a sedate contentment.

In the fall, the leaves turned brown, orange and gold, and the air cooled off. The world took on a more introspective mood; as yet unhampered by the burdens of adulthood. I still feel this in the fall. Fall and spring are my favorite times of the year.

Winters in Wisconsin were hard in the days before global warming. Bitterly cold. Waist deep snow. Driving icy winds hammering at us from Lake Michigan. Violent and frightening storms would erupt on the lake during the Gales of November. But this didn't seem to spoil the beauty of the land. It had a song of its own: if you knew how to listen.

All this was thrown into raw, sharp relief. In the field and in the swamp. Near the field was a small shopping mall. One of the first of its kind in the area. It had a grocery store, drug store, hardware store, liquor store, and two other small businesses that changed from time to time.

In later years the shopping mall began to grow. On the opposite side of the field, they began to build low income housing. Bulldozers and diggers came and began to dig up pieces of the field. *Our field!* When we realized that they were taking away our field, we retaliated as best as we knew how. Needless to say, we didn't succeed in stopping them. They finished the buildings.

Then they began building more, and more. They drained the swamp, and paved it over. The birds and frogs that lived there died. The mosquitoes that they ate overpopulated and in the summer clouds of them were everywhere. Entire species of insects disappeared. I haven't seen a stag beetle in decades. They upset the balance of nature, and nobody noticed. Nobody cared. Someone was making money: and the rest were sold the lie of impending prosperity that never came.

By this time I was beginning to be distracted by the peculiar sensation of entry into young adulthood.

Later, I moved to New York City. I got lost in the concrete jungle.

The field is gone. The swamp is gone. The children have no

place to play. Nowhere to be human.

These are my memories, my treasures. You can't take them from me.

A Delicious Madness

Wandering through the desert night,

No guide but my homesickness.

I scream my frustration at the stars,

Spit curses at the moon,

And throw rocks at Venus.

"How could you treat me like this?

Why do you enjoy causing me so much pain?"

They answer with a silence that deafens me.

I look around;

Nothing in either direction.

I am lost.

I sink to my knees and cry to the heavens;

"Is union found in the longing?

Am I a beggar, running through the streets crying the name of his

Beloved?

Or am I a blind fool, who franticly searches the world for what

rests firmly in his right hand?"

O Beloved!!

You dragged me over the horizon and under the earth till my eyes

bled;

My brain boiled and torn to pieces by too much reality;

Too much inside me that I never offered to You.

Longing for my Lover to take me and burn me away if I tried to

stay

Or crawl inside my gallery of self-imagined idols and attempting to
pray
without being Drunk on Your Wine.
How could I be so stupid?
I strut about thinking myself bold
Breathing my own wonder
Yet living in the dung-oven of my own foolishness.
Oh Lover! What is the Shape of Light?
Trickling grains of sand
Rise like the sun and drop like rain
I panic, and cry to the heavens;
"Why? What?"
And the answer that was waiting there before I was born:
"Turn the hourglass, you fool!"

The moon sets.
The stars fade.
The sun rises and burns away the night's madness.
The journey continues.

The Shari'ah and What Humbles It.

And now, a question terrifying and inevitable we must ask;

Of what use is Shari'ah if it produces no spiritual result?

The Shariah is the pool of Bethesda.

Its water a medicine that we must enter and drink.

The Shari'ah is the rope that bound Ulysses,

and the wax that filled his men's ears as they passed the realm of
the Sirens.

The wax, a veil protecting them from what they could not bear,

the rope allowing the stronger of them to hear that song, and
survive.

Love is the cord that binds the universe.

Love is the indestructible axis around which all things revolve.

Hanifi could write no fiqh about love.

Shafi'i had nothing to say about it.

Bukhari was stunned into silence.

What words could they say to equal the Voice crying out from the

desert, the burning bush, the Mountain of Light?

The songs that are sung by joyful stars,

And the dance of Laughing Lions?

Madness overshadows us!

Every rock, every wall, every tree,

Every galaxy, every atom, every wave, every particle

Reminds up of what we seek;

And the single tear shed for love,

Has more wealth and power than all the oceans.

An Open Letter to ISIS.

I grew up near Lake Michigan and am a good swimmer. The lake is beautiful. Nonetheless I go into the water when the waves are big, the sea is gray and the wind is blowing violently. Fishermen stay onshore and the lifeguard hoists the red flag to warn people. I ignore them. A part of me wishes to perish in the howling infinite of the ocean. But only when I am brave and my vision is clear.

By hammering a narrow vision of Islam on the heads of others, you are a red flag telling them to stay away from the ocean their hearts desire.

What does this mean? You will never understand.

It's been years since I began to walk this Path. I learned a lot. Listening to those who falsely claim lineage to the Salaf pulls people away from Islam and gives space to haunting doubts that lurk in the mind.

Every tyrant throughout history has built an army. They always do it the same way: find poor, uneducated, frustrated, disenfranchised young men, tell them how "special" they are, and hand them weapons. It works every time. It worked with you; but we all know that many of these people are - how shall I say it? - "connected." (*Nudge, nudge, wink, wink*)

It is beautiful to embrace and being embraced by Allah; but your way is the way of the rapist and the plunderer. I am not having it!!

Still, I had a vision. It was a vision in the form of a dream.

I saw a light on the peak of a mountain and climbed there with little effort. When I arrived, I could not get over the final precipice on my own efforts. Two beings; a male and a female, young, very beautiful, helped me. Even though they were not strong enough to pull me up; our combined efforts got me over the final edge. An old man covered with the cloak of initiation was on the peak, and waited to greet me. But the peak was not a peak: it was a vast, wide house. I was welcomed into a warm, comfortable place, and given food. A gathering of the elders of my tribe were in the great hall, engaged in a beautiful statement of remembrance.

The Master of my heart said: "My religion is vast; much more so than the cold didactic of those who clothe their legalistic idolatry in shrouds of false righteousness. Do not listen to them. This is your beautiful inheritance! Go and explore".

The elders waited for me, until the food had strengthened me. The man who had welcomed me gave me instructions, and disappeared

Something else happened; but you cannot understand.

Now I tell you this: because of your words and actions I was saddened beyond measure. But then again, maybe I should thank you for your clumsy, idiotic tyranny after all.

A Bright Moment.

(This is a short story version of an earlier edit of a chapter from my first novel A Quantum Hijra.)

Two years had passed since Talib had joined the Order. Talib, a friend of his named Yusef, Hassan, Sheikh Suliman, Jamal, Zeinab, Tchikako, and Maryam were having coffee in a coffee shop a mere seven blocks away from the chasm where the World Trade Center had once stood. Nevertheless, it – and the equally aesthetically displeasing buildings that were being erected in its place - failed to dampen the mood of the group, which was lighthearted and. This was to be one of those gatherings that would bring wondrous intellectual and philosophical discussions to fruition.

He was finding that his new level of awareness was not as he expected it would be. There was room for laughter, for example. At first this puzzled him. But he realized that piety and enlightenment can be pleasurable.

The stories he'd been hearing about the behavior of Sufi mystics; ancient and modern, were beginning to make sense. He saw a pattern in their lives, and the hidden meaning behind the incomprehensible things they said and did. Hassan knew this was happening, as did Sheikh Suliman. Both men recognized the changes that were wrought in the rapidly enlightened young man. Sheikh Suliman saw everything at a glance: the whole of Talib's life and struggle was an open book to him.

Yet, despite the lighthearted mood, the air about the group seemed intellectually charged.

They'd been talking about religion.

"Now, and you know," Zeinab postulated, "the truth is that the Torah, Nevium, and Gospels are not in their pure form anymore."

"What kills me," interjected Yusef, "is that the Jews are always going on and on about their being 'God's Chosen People'. But look at what happened in their history. Their own Scriptures say that they rejected God in favor of idolatry when they worshiped the golden calf. I think it was, ahh, where was that? Oh yeah! Exodus 32:1-10. And this was AFTER they saw all of those miracles that Moses (as) performed, Masha Allah. The fact that they received the Law eventually meant next to nothing because the Bani Israel broke their covenant with God over and over again, sometimes even killing their Prophets! In the Qur'an, the Children of Israel are admonished for having violated their Covenant with God. Check out Surat-ul Bani Israel 7:2-9. I was telling a Jew the other day that the Qur'an only admonishes Jews in those instances where they violated their covenant."

Talib said "I had a conversation with a Zionist Rabbi. He looked me in the eye and told me that since God wants the Jews to have the Holy land, and it's not only permissible but necessary for the Jews to exterminate the Palestinians! Do you believe that?"

"Yo, check it out," Yusef said. "I read that in the Talmud, it says all kinds of stuff. Like; 'Jehovah created the non-Jew in human form so that the Jew would not have to be served by beasts. The non-Jew is consequently an animal in human form and condemned to serve the Jew day and night', 'The Jews are human beings, but the nations of the world are not human beings but beasts', 'Murdering Goyim is like killing a wild animal', 'G-d has given the Jews power over the possessions and blood of all nations', 'Do not save Goyim in danger of death. Show no mercy to the Goyim'. Jews are not treated this badly in any Islamic Scripture, even when they are being reprimanded by Allah. Allah calls Jews and Christians "The People of the Book" a title of great nobility! Islamic Law forbids Muslims from violating the human and civil rights of Jews and Christians. There were times when the Prophet Muhammad (sas) was required to render judgment in disputes between Jews and Muslims, and when it served justice and piety he ruled in favor of the Jews. I can't find where Jewish Law makes such guarantees to non-Jews. I don't understand how the Zionists expect the Gentiles to cheerfully submit to chattel slavery."

"Yeah," Talib said. "Look at what happened with Palestine. The Nazis tried to exterminate the Jews, and then after the war, they founded Israel and did the same thing to the Palestinians that the Nazis did to them."

Maryam said "I have a book at home, called *Zionist Relations with Nazi Germany* by a man named Faris Glubb. He put all kind of evidence in there to prove that the Nazis collaborated with the Zionists in Europe to pull off the holocaust."

"The Christians are no better," Yusef went on. "Most of them don't know that the Nician Council of 325 a.d. when they chose the books of the Bible was lead by the Roman emperor Constantine. He was a pagan who murdered his wife and first born son. Now, when the original Gospels were gathered, Constantine ordered that they all be translated into Greek, and that the original Hebrew and Aramaic be destroyed.

Possession of a copy of any Gospel in Hebrew or Aramaic was punishable by death. One of them that survived was the Gospel of Barnabas. I think he was buried with it. It was not only written by an actual eyewitness of Jesus ministry but corresponds with Qur'anic revelation and even mentions Muhammad by name: the "Comforter" Jesus spoke of in John 14:26. The Christians think it means 'Holy Ghost.' They changed the English word 'Comforter' for the Greek 'Paraclytos' (Paraclete in Latin). The Gospel of John was in Greek, but Jesus spoke Aramaic. The Aramaic word for Paraclytos is 'Ahmed,' which translates into Arabic as 'Muhammad.'"

Yusef said "Yeah, I know about that. There were all these different sects of early Christians. The Arian sect taught that Jesus was divine yet distinct from, and inferior to God. The Sabellians taught that Jesus was an aspect of God. The Trinitarians taught that God, Jesus, and the Holy Spirit were three in one and one in three. But check it out: in 1957, a committee was formed consisting of 33 of the world's most eminent Christian scholars from 17 cooperating denominations to examine the most ancient of Biblical manuscripts and translate them into what would be the Standard Revised Version of the Bible. In the course of their work they found that the First Epistle of John 5:7, and another one, ah,, somewhere toward the end of Matthew; the only references to the Holy Trinity in the entire Bible, were forgeries that were not in the original texts. So they threw them out. But in 1971, after years of pressure from the Church, the verses were reinstated."

Sheikh Suliman, who had been listening to this discourse with tolerance, waved his hand to silence the group. All heads turned and looked at him.

He was silent for several seconds. Nobody dared break the silence.

Finally, he spoke. "Self-righteous anger is a dangerous drug," he said, in a quiet but authoritative voice. "It causes us to forget that all religious bigotry begins with the error of mistaking the map for the territory; and in the ego wanting to make itself a false idol."

Nobody could respond. Instead, they sipped their coffee in sheepish silence.

After a moment of quiet introspection, they changed the subject. The conversation turned to fortune tellers.

"In my days of jahaliyah," said Sheikh Suliman, "I used to practice ritual magick, especially the school of thought founded by Aleister Crowley. I belonged to several orders and meddled in all manner of things. I was very good a reading tarot cards. I understood what each card was and how they interacted."

"I did a little research on the tarot," Hassan said. "Each card was originally the page of a book that corresponded to the Qabbalah, wasn't it?"

"Yes," said Sheikh Suliman. "It goes back the Ancient Egyptian Mystery School, and has cross references to astrology. Each card or page represented a path or sphere on the Qabbalistic Tree of life. There are 72 in all.

"The problem is that most people fail to see that each of these 72 spheres and paths are merely steps. None of them is an end in itself. And really, the tarot, the I Ching, and whatever else, are nothing more than random symbol generators. It's like the Hadith where the Prophet (sas) said that his people would divide into 72 sects and that all but one would be destined for hellfire. This is part of the interpretation of that Hadith, stopping at any particular level of the Path. There is a deeper warning against becoming lost in that which is not No-Thing. There is no stasis on the Path; you either grow or degenerate. As you can imagine, the Hadith about the 72 sects was taken by many superficial people as license to condemn all sects but their own. People easily become enslaved by forms and shadows from the disharmony that pollutes the hearts of men and djinn. We see evidence of this all around us. The 'sects' are just condensations of these 72 paths on the Qabbalistic Tree of Life that, if seen as ends in themselves, divert us from the Straight Path. At the top of the Tree of Life, the last sphere is not widely understood to be a gateway itself. The realm beyond it is translated from Hebrew into English as 'No-Thing'. Do you remember Ayat-ul Kursi in the Qur'an? Do you know that the Tao Ti Chieng said 'The Tao that can be known is not the true Tao'?

Zeinab looked up from her coffee, which was becoming cold. "But I thought the old religions had it wrong."

"There is some truth to that," Sheikh Suliman said. "But there are many things in them if you know where to look, and how to interpret them. Gotama Buddha attained enlightenment under the Lotus tree. But do you remember the Prophet's (sas) Night Journey? He went beyond the Lotus tree, into the realm that neither the Buddha nor Gibreel could reach. All the pre-Islamic religions and Revelations were components of a process. That process was completed with the Qur'an and the Prophet

Muhammad (sas)."

Tchikako said "I remember two things from when I was reading about Zen. One of them was the saying 'He who has attained supreme illumination is like an arrow flying into hell'. The other was when a Zen master announced that one of the students, so & so, had attained illumination. The other students went to him and asked how he felt now that he was illuminated. He said 'as miserable as ever.'"

When the laughter ebbed, Sheikh Suliman said "The idols cling to their lives. Creation involves a condensation of the Spirit into the corporeal, and then it's inevitable return. There are stages, stations, to this cyclical process, and dangers along the Path. These things cannot be correctly understood except through Qur'anic Revelation. Without it, they are fragmented and incomplete, and present a danger that haunts us at every step of the way."

He paused, sipping his coffee in silence. "An ancient Muslim mystic said 'If people knew what Islam was really all about, they'd become idol worshipers.' Now, statements like this are not to be taken literally, of course. Like Mansur al-Halajj saying 'I am the Truth.' As you recall, they hung him. As we advance, we see new levels of understanding in this. But you can't say this to everyone, unless your Faith is strong enough to withstand being called and treated like a heretic. Or worse."

Hassan said "There is within all the Scriptures an inner truth. In some, it was obscured by psychological archetype that we have little reference points for. Some are mathematical allegory. Some, like what we find in the Torah, Nevium, and canonic Gospels, are deliberate human alteration. It's tragic that most people have neither desire nor capacity for intellectual and spiritual achievement. Yet my former disdain for such people begins to dissipate. There is a Big Picture, and they have their place in the structure that the picture points to."

He took a sip of his coffee. "Have you ever read the Bhagavad Gita? Of course you have. There was a moment where Krishna's friend Arjuna was defeated. He was the greatest warrior in the world, and stood on a battlefield facing an army that had relatives, uncles, cousins, and brothers ready to slaughter him. Muhammad (sas) faced the same situation at the battles of Badr and Uhud. Now, on the surface, it would seem that he was crushed by having to raise his bow and arrows against his family. But there is a greater truth behind that.

He was facing not his flesh and blood relatives; but the truths concealed within his own heart. And those truths are held behind barriers of fear. And we can only conquer that fear by entering it head on. Otherwise we are fighting nothing but shadows, phantoms. We can spend our lives hacking away at that million headed hydra until we rot, and we will achieve nothing. There is only one battleground, and one enemy of the Light within us: the heart. Arjuna saw that, and that's what defeated him. It was only Krishna's guidance that caused him to rise and do what he had to do.

"Most people cannot face this. Most cannot see past the million headed hydra, let alone even face that phantom. Nietzsche knew this; even if his explanations were not easy to understand."

"Well, maybe a new kind of religious society could rise up," Maryam said. "Something that would fix the problems we have and help people get closer to the Light."

"I doubt that a 'new church' is the answer to our problem" Hassan said. "In the end it will solve nothing. What, apart from an actual transformation of humanity, an apotheosis, would prevent the exact same problems that have arisen for centuries? Nothing, and we all know it. The interplay between politics and orthodox religion is unavoidable and inevitable. That power struggle permeates the training, educating, disciplining, and establishing of the orthodox community. All leaders of such bodies inevitably face the ultimate question: whether to succumb to complete opportunism as the price of maintaining their rule, or sacrifice everything to the underlying religious ethic. Most chose the former, on the pretext of acquiring power 'temporarily' in order to safeguard the environment wherein the religious ethic may flourish. This is a lie they tell themselves and believe.

"Its like Ibn Arabi said in the Fusus al-hikam 'Some only ride on paths, while others rise across trackless deserts. Those who ride on paths appear like those who can see the way to Allah. Those who ride across trackless deserts, appear like those who have lost the way to Allah. Yet Allah reveals Himself within the souls of both; he is the inner reality of all people.' *Appear*: that's the word that tells us what he really meant! Or when the Prophet (sas) said 'Sometimes you will meet those who appear to be the people of the Garden, when they are really the people of Hellfire; and those who appear to be the people of Hellfire who are really the people of the Garden.'

"The point," Hassan continued, "is that people have different ways by which the Mystery is revealed to them. Ours is music. We stand at the barrier between two worlds. We are the doorway, the fulcrum of spiritual events. In the end, we, like all people, will face reality alone, but we had a foretaste of it. Allah is merciful!"

The group fell into silence. Some turned their attention to a TV screen, where CNN was re-running the day's headlines.

Hassan said "We're all slaves, you know."

"What do you mean?" asked Tchikako. "I thought Lincoln abolished slavery."

Hassan chuckled. "Yeah, well, when the Federal Reserve Act was signed, the US government handed its economic power to a private bank. What happened was that the US couldn't pay back the money that was owed. So, they imposed Admiralty Law upon the citizens. That's where birth certificates come from. Any certificate, by definition, establishes ownership. What? Did you think you needed to prove that you were born? Hell no. It's a warehouse certificate. The US put up its own citizens as collateral against a loan and interest it could never pay back. The US went bankrupt in, when was that? March of 1933 I think."

"That sucks." said Tchikako.

"Does it ever!" added Zeinab. "Everyone with a birth certificate is property. A slave. Lincoln never freed anybody!"

"You're a lawyer; you ought to know," said Talib.

Zeinab glanced at him, and went on. "The language of these certificates and laws are designed to describe a person not as a sentient entity that Allah created with free will. It describes us as corporations. When we sign or accept them, we indirectly accept being classified as a corporation that the stipulations of the constitution no longer apply to. Look at your driver's license. Your name is in all capital letters. This is a legal procedure called '*capitis diminuto maximus*.' This legally turns a human being into an artificial entity. But the thing is that 'us" and 'them' are two different and distinct societies. They use language most people don't understand to hide the one relevant fact from us; we are not answerable to them."

Jamal said "True, dat. But then they send mean stupid men with guns to do their dirty work."

"The whole thing is an act of the divisive and dividing ego." Zeinab said. "These 'societies' – or the divisive and dividing ego for that matter - are really a cancerous growth upon humanity. It acts exactly like a parasite. Any parasite needs to leech its sustenance from the host body. It actually floods the body with chemical messages that tell the body it craves what the parasite needs to survive, and starving itself. In this case, that sustenance is our conscious energy. And the chemical message is fear. That fear requires us to divert energy away from more productive endeavors. The parasite creates more and more fear, and convinces the host that it and it alone can protect the host. Fear of autonomy is very important for the parasite; because without the participation of the host body the parasite cannot survive."

"Shaitan is a parasite." Tchikako said simply.

"Yes," Talib said. "The name 'Shaitan' has its root in the word for the divisive and dividing ego."

"And it's with the cancer that is killing humanity. We are permitting this to happen. All the so called 'leaders' and 'powers that be' need our conscious participation and psychic energy. Without it, they starve. Their nature depends entirely upon the people's desire to be ruled. And we're in denial over this. We think we're free, but we are more enslaved than ever. And for every tyranny that falls, another will rise to replace it, so long as humanity fails to see that the root of this is found within the Jungian collective unconscious."

"Why do we have such trouble seeing what's happening?" Tchikako asked.

"Because of the repression of acknowledgment of those lower qualities of ourselves, and of human free will." Sheikh Suliman said. "We deny the symptoms of our spiritual diseases, and the facts about our own true nature. And we deny human free will. Not 'desire.' That's something else entirely; and has nothing to do with will. The root of evil lies in self-hatred – no less than in envy. This is a rage originating in a self-betrayal that begins in childhood, when autonomy is surrendered in exchange for the "love" of those who wield power over us. You know; schools, bullies, police, governments, etc. To share in that subjugating power, people create a false self, a pleasing-to-others image of themselves that springs from a powerful, deep-seated fear of being hurt, humiliated or abandoned. This pattern of over-adaptation, and the fate of those who resist the pressure to conform, can be traced to this. But the insanity and detachment that this hyper-conformity produces, is not widely known because it has become the cold, tough "realism" that modern society inculcates into its members and even admires.

"Now, simple rebellion is not the way to escape from these patterns. Rebels often remain emotionally tied to the objects of their rebellion, and feeds hearts full of vicious intentions. This is why revolutionaries always become despotic administrators.

"What we need to development is a personal autonomy, and to avoid all forms of self-deception. Autonomy and authenticity are not easily attained. But without them, our efforts will be catastrophic to both individual and society. Because more and more embittered conformists will come out of the shadows to seek new victims on whom to wreak violence and avenge their psychic wounds. Hell is an abyss where we face ourselves. People are terrified by the idea of facing themselves, and will go to any extreme to avoid this. Because when people have no external object to identify their darkness with, they are forced to recognize it as part of themselves; and have no way to cope with it. We are surrounded by such people, and their energies and the results of their actions are like a suffocating cloud we find difficulty escaping from.

"There can only be one government that will work; the government of individual autonomy. The government of no government. The goal is for the Murids to *think and feel;* and see a plethora of ways as opposed to a fixed government / media / clan approved direction. This is a sound strategy to understand the Prophetic Language of Dhikr as opposed to the intellectual slavery and impotence of the Middle Eastern Muslim groups and weak Sufi tariqas. The Prophet (sas) said that he who knows himself knows his Rabb. This being true, humanity does not know itself, does not want to know itself, and by default allows the madness in this dunyah to continue. No government can ever work; there are no political solutions; only political problems. It is only by the refinement of the soul though true knowledge of self and the cultivation of autonomous free will that the world and we, the custodians of our world, bodies, and minds, will survive and prosper."

After a moment of silence, Tchikako said "That's deep."

"It's only common sense." Sheikh Suliman said. "A rare element indeed!" Everyone chuckled.

Hassan said "This is where real power lies. Not in politics; but in the refinement of the spirit. It even affects the dunyah in ways nobody can resist. Nobody but dusty old historians knows who King George III was, but everyone recognizes Handel's "Messiah." At the premiere of the piece, the king wept, in public. Who had the real power?"

Just then, the song "Up From the Skies" by Jimi Hendrix filled the air.

"This" Talib said as the song played "was one of the most dangerous songs Hendrix ever did."

Maryam looked at him, nonplussed, and said "Huh?"

"Oh, sure; there were others. Like that line in the long version of 'Voodoo Chile' where he said something about being by the methane sea, which was later confirmed by the Cassini – Hugyens mission to Titan. But 'Up from the Skies' talks all kinds of uncomfortable things that a very few people don't want us to know about, and which most people would prefer to be blind about."

Tchicako, still confused, said "I don't get it."

"OK. Hendrix started by letting people know that what he's going to talk about is probably pretty heavy stuff; but don't worry, I'm not trying to hurt you. Now, this is where it gets heavy. He first places himself completely outside the flow of human history. He's a visitor, and observer. And as an impartial observer, he sees the human race as a 'people farm.' This is the most disturbing thing he could have said. There are legends, myths, and arcane traditions from a wide variety of sources that say, in a nutshell, that the human race is under the control of a race of non-corporeal demonic entities that feed off of our psychic energies. They use the oligarchy to control the world, and even to instigate mass slaughter, which releases massive amounts of energy that they feed off of. Human sorcerers can also harvest this kind of energy. This is the real reason why there are wars on the scale that we have them. Only the most evolved human beings can protect themselves from this race of parasites, and their human servants. The energy that our evolved people develop confuses and repels these demonic things. I'm sure you've hears these stories."

They all nodded their heads. They'd heard many of them.

Talib said "There's more truth in them than most people would dare admit, even for the sake of argument. We have an internal loathing and revulsion of these entities. Most are not strong enough to even think about this. Only Allah and His gifts to us can protect us from being livestock.

Sheikh Suliman muttered "By foulness shall ye know them."

"But anyway," Talib said "back to the Hendrix song. Next he refers to the whole family of humanity, and the cold cruelty with which they treat each other. Hendrix, in the role of the outside observer, is amazed at this. Then he refers to the untapped potential of the human mind, the resources we have and are not even aware of. He asks if we know that we were, indeed once noble and highly evolved beings, but had lost our own greatness."

Zeinab said "Well, we did 'fall' didn't we? A lot of religions say that."

"Yeah" Talib said. "And we don't really know everything about that story, do we? And even in this Hendrix may have subtly tapped into something. Then he talks about being here before, when there was an ice age; and perhaps this could refer to the lost civilization of Atlantis. Many people believe Atlantis was where Antarctica is now; and that part of the disaster that destroyed them was a shift in the earth's polarity. This will happen again, by the way. Perhaps it will happen sooner than we think.

"He goes on to talking about stuff that we're now beginning to suspect may happen to the world.

"Allah is best to know. But we see signs. And he ends by saying that he wants to know about 'the new mother earth', and he wants to see and hear everything. A renewed world, and to know everything; to once again know the names of all the things in creation, like Adaam, alyhi asalaam, did."

"Damn!" Yusef said.

"Yes. And what about the name of the album this song is on: "Axis: Bold as Love'? If this isn't a reference to the Qtub, well, again, Allah is best to know."

Tchicako asked "Qtub? I'm not familiar with that."

Hassan said "It means 'Axis' - a central figure, a person, who is responsible for the reintroduction of religious truth as society and psychological associations change throughout the ages. Such are necessary for the existence of the world, and who who provides a focus for spiritual teachings. I can't explain how Hendrix was aware of this."

Taking a sip of coffee, Talib continued "I recently got my hands on an unreleased song Hendrix did called "Valley of Neptune." I heard they plan on releasing it in 2010 or thereabouts. In that song he sings about a coming natural disaster. Something about the rising and falling of civilizations, massive changes in the earth itself, and in the destiny of humanity. No wonder they pulled the plug on our friend Jimi. May Allah forgive him and grant him peace."

Talib sighed. "There's something else about that whole period of time. The 60s, I mean. Think about this. The Vietnam War started in 1964, when the Navy pulled a 'false / false flag' move in the Gulf of Tonkin. Congress passed the Tonkin Gulf Resolution, and the Vietnam War was underway."

Zeinab said "What do you mean, 'false / false flag?"

"OK: I'm making up words again. The truth is, a false flag is when the government or military rigs a faked attack to justify a response. In Tonkin, there never was an attack. The Navy tried to provoke a defensive response, which they'd spin into as an unprovoked attack on U.S ships. But when Vietnamese forces didn't react, Uncle Sam decided to just pretend it happened, and they started the war. But let me get back to the point I was making. The man in charge of the whole operation was Admiral George Stephen Morrison."

"And you bring him up because,,, " Zeinab interjected.

"Because of his son" Talib said. "His son was Jim Morrison, the singer of the Doors."

"What?"

"Yes. The Lizard King is descended from a powerful military family. But it doesn't end there; all kind of people from the hippie / peace / flower power movement were from powerful families. 'Papa' John Phillips, Stephen Stills, David Crosby, Jackson Browne, the members of that group America, Gram Parsons, Frank Zappa, and even Zappa's wife Gail came from a powerful military family. 'Papa' John Philips married Susie Adams, a direct descendant of John Adams, one of the 'Founding Fathers' of the US. David Crosby is also a direct descendant of Alexander Hamilton, and related to the Van Cortlandt, Van Schuyler and Van Rensselaer families. There were others. Hendrix' manager, Michael Jeffery, was a former officer with British military intelligence. Mike Nesmith of the Monkees came to LA after time with the U.S. Air Force, joined the Monkees, and later inherited a family fortune estimated at $25 million. And the weird thing is that they all had something else in common. They all were part of a community based in Laurel Canyon in Los Angeles. The point is, the 'hippie'/anti-war crowd was born in that little area, and spread from there.

"They all gathered almost simultaneously to Laurel Canyon. But at the time, there wasn't much of a pop music industry or live pop music scene to speak of in Los Angeles. There was no logical reason for them to do so. It would have made sense these days for them to go to Nashville, Detroit, New York, or London. It wasn't the industry that attracted these people. It was the Laurel Canyon crowd that transformed Los Angeles into the epicenter of the music industry. And they defined the whole hippie / flower child thing."

Tchikako said "So, wait; what's your point?"

"The point is that the leaders of the governments saw, with Elvis Presley and the Beatles, that the unprecedented mass appeal of the new music gave the singers a voice in public affairs. They couldn't let this evolve outside of their control. And around '64, '65, there was a strong anti-war movement gaining momentum. They were well organized, had a coherent intelligencia, and posed a real opposition to what the US was doing in Southeast Asia. This is the point; the unwashed, drug-addled long-hairs sporting flowers and peace symbols was far easier to marginalize, or even eliminate, than respected college professors and their students. They couldn't affect anything. I mean, look at the number of these folks, and their girlfriends, wives, managers, and whatnot, who come from a similar background. It was as if an overwhelming majority of the kids from that era who had musical talent were the sons and daughters of Navy Admirals, chemical warfare engineers and Air Force intelligence officers; and were among the only ones who were signed to lucrative recording contracts and promoted by their labels and the media."

Tchicako looked at him. "You're saying that the hippie movement was engineered to prevent the anti-war movement from becoming too powerful?"

"Yes," Talib said "Think about it. If they were rebelling against, rather than promoting, the values of their parents, then why didn't they ever speak out against the people they were rebelling against? Why didn't Jim Morrison mention the fact that his father was responsible for starting an illegal war? Frank Zappa never wrote a song about the horrors of chemical warfare, even though his father worked to develop chemical weapons. No Mamas and Papas song denounced the values and actions of Phillips' family. David Crosby and Stephen Stills never disowned the family values that they were raised with. And even though they were supposedly part of the whole anti-establishment, anti-capitalism thing, they made lots of money."

"Look" Tchicacko said "Morrison could have just been trying to distance himself from his family. And he was a drunkard and a lunatic anyway. Same thing with Zappa. Maybe they didn't want to attract attention to that part of their lives."

"Oh yeah, Morrison was bat manure crazy. No argument there." Talib said. "But despite some overlapping, the 'hippie'/'flower child' movement was never the same as the anti-war movement, even though it was subliminally promoted as such by the mass media. There were no hippies at the March on Washington in '65. And consider the presumably virtuous musicians who were subjected to FBI CoIntelPro harassment and/or assassinated by the CIA. Bottom line; the hippies that were spawned from that collective in Laurel Canyon created a subculture that inhibited the anti-war movement by absorbing potential numbers into an ideology that rendered them completely impotent. The CIA probably brought LSD into the anti-war movement to turn potential protesters and resistors into self-absorbed burnouts. Abbie Hoffman and activists like the Berkeley radicals and the White Panthers who were trying to stop the war and change the status quo hated the flower children. They were spoiled children who were only interested in drugs and sex. And LSD wasn't like peyote or ayahuasca, with centuries of tradition as a ritualistic tool. It was just dumped on them, with no idea how to use it to enhance their quest for truth. It did the job of frying their brains like hamburgers and neutralizing the potential threat they posed to the war effort.

"And what was the music that was promoted in the years that followed when the flower child movement went sour? Faceless corporate rock, new wave, and disco. Even the drugs of choice during these decades, cocaine, heroin, crack, meth, and the like couldn't even pretend to be 'visionary' or inspiring.'"

Tchicako said "You realize this all sounds a little paranoid." She paused. "But you're right about one thing, we humans have more within us than meets the eye. Hendrix told us that in his music, and so did a lot of others. People don't realize that we are not just chunk of meat walking around; and there are people who don't want us to change."

Talib said "And then you got the Wahabbis who are always trying to prove that music is forbidden. You read what Sheikh Suliman wrote in the Order's book. The Hadiths used by the Wahabbi-influenced Muslims to argue that music and musical instruments are forbidden are not authentic."

"Wait," Maryam said "How do you know those Hadiths are not authentic?"

Jamal interjected "One of the sub-narrators, Hisham ibn Amaar, was the break in the chain of transmission. Bukhari, Abu Dawood, Ibn Kathir, Imam Hanbali, Imam Hanifah, and several others all said his testimony was worthless. That alone should prove it's not authentic. But it doesn't matter. I stopped wanting to argue about this long ago,"

Tchicako said "It's just another thing people use because they don't want us to know our full potential. They want to control our art because they don't want any competition in trying to own everything and rule everyone."

Hassan said "Even science knows that we are a repository of untapped potential. The primary function of human DNA is not in protein synthesis, but in electromagnetic energy reception and transmission. I think only three percent of the function of DNA deal with protein, the rest deals with bioacoustics and bioelectrical signaling. And the heart and the brain are always talking to each other. They send messages to each other all the time. The heart sends more information to the brain than the brain sends to the heart; and it influences all kinds of things like perception, cognition, emotional processing, that kind of stuff. Our heart generates a rhythmic electromagnetic field that can be measured in the brain waves of people around us. It affects cells, water and DNA all around us. Our bodies are talking to each other and sending signals – I think it's called 'morphic resonance.'"

"And all this ties in with the primordia of matter and energy"

"Yeah," Jamal interjected. "It's like with those old civilizations. They used art and ritual as technology. It was the cornerstone of their civilizations. The Egyptians took it so seriously that individual artistic expression was unheard of, which is whack, if you ask me. But the idea of using art for a reason was what these guys were all about. They used it to reach into their psyches and introduce what was in the subconscious to the conscious. And it was all tied in to nature. But then they let it become idolatry. I don't think it was that in the beginning. It was only technology they used to understand the universe, and themselves. In the Gnostic Injeel, Isa ibn Maryam (as) said something like 'If you bring forth what is within you, it will save you, and if you do not, what you don't bring forth will destroy you.' So it's important to know what we really are."

Sheikh Suliman said "Ibn Arabi once said, "And only from the Law of Tajalli upon a mirror, emerges our knowledge about the 'difference' between the viewer the mirror and the image formed upon the mirror!"

"Polish the mirror of your soul!" said Talib.

"Yeah," Yusef said. "Which brings up the idea of the reflected and reflection. It's like 'difference' only has meaning on our transient temporal side of the universe. The image might be of some other object than that of the viewer, like if you hold a mirror and you might see your face or tilt it and see the image of other objects around the room."

` "There is a Quantal Reflection off of a barrier, like a mirror, that is related to a Sufi concept of the foundation for 'I.'" said Sheikh Suliman. "You ever hear about it? In Richard Feynman's PhD thesis as well as his QT original formulation he pretty much outlined how 'I' is a Quantal Reflection off of a chiral barrier. But 'I's Quantum Mechanics has no wave-function! It's the 'Tunnel Effect'; A particle , i.e. words, thoughts, acts, etc, leaving the human Wujud / Being aiming at the other universe, some part of the existence of the Wujud, the 'particle' cannot penetrate the barrier, But the wave aspect, some of it penetrates, and the rest is reflected back towards the human Wujud, and humanity and the whole universe. You might have said that the said barrier is a half-mirror, partly allows for the words to get through and partly reflects the words."

Hassan said "But Feynman's chiral formulations cannot have a simple Hamiltonian time-evolution equations since the particle acts upon itself from the past and from the future! 'I' being thought of as a reflection off a Quantal barrier, thus must share the same formulation attribute i.e. 'I' cannot be modeled by any Hamiltonian-like equation. This shows the difference between the human being and the monkey. The monkey traverses linearly through time as opposed to the non-Hamiltonian progression of us human beings. I wonder if this explains the difference of behavior between a human facing a mirror and that of a monkey."

"Look," said Sheikh Suliman. "'I's passage through time being Quantal, and given the chiral effect, cannot be expressed via a wave-function; the best formulation currently available would be transitional probabilities from one region of space-time to another or from one state to another. The Sufi concept is recognized as transition from Hala - a Momentary state - to another Hala. I guess that's the best we can formulate for the inner workings of 'I' and its passage through time.

"And there are also many ambient additions to 'I.' The image of a face reflected from a mirror has many artifacts integrated into it, like your face is formed into a reflected image off the mirror, plus all the objects around you in the frame of the mirror's capacity to reflect. So 'I' reflected off the chiral barrier reflects much more than our original Wujud. This shows the incompleteness of the Probability and 'I'. If the probability's formal system was complete, then the I's Ambiance would not seamlessly fit with the 'I' as an inherent part of 'I'. If it was complete, and it was articulating propositions about the 'I' reflection, then any ambient addition would either need new axioms added to the probability's formal system, or the ambient add-ons would immediately be rejected by the mind and thus the reflected image of 'I' discarded as a 'myself' or gross inconsistencies would have been noted at all times.

Hassan said "Don't forget the Feynman-Stueckelberg interpretation. By considering the propagation of the negative energy modes of the electron field backward in time, Ernst Stueckelberg found a pictorial understanding of the particle and antiparticle having equal mass m and spin J but opposite charges q. That way, he could rewrite perturbation theory precisely in the form of diagrams. Feynman later made his own systematic derivation of these diagrams from particle formalism, and they are now called Feynman diagrams. Each line of a diagram represents a particle propagating either backward or forward in time. This is how they compute amplitudes in quantum field theory. These guys needed antiparticles so that their equations would work to exist with the particles at the same time, they need to move in reverse-time! With a linear model of time we see the time's behavior is not a simple flow or river type, it's really complicated."

"You all are giving me a headache!" Maryam exclaimed. "What does all this have to do with Sufism and Divine Love?"

"Everything," said Sheikh Suliman. "No Fana - Evanescence, dissolving into the Beloved - is possible if the probability's formal system is complete. Incompleteness of the probability's formal system allows for articulation of cut-and-paste universes where a universe containing 'I' can be glued to one containing no-I, and yet due to incompleteness, the probability theory could still articulate statements about both the universes.

"When there was no way to reach and find Allah, it was the same time when the human being / lover disappeared from the realm of the souls; and when the we appeared in this world, a mirror appeared in the other world that reflected only the Nur (Divine Light) from Allah and none else. It was reflecting the absence of the lover; and when that mirror of sanctification appeared 'There' a mirror appeared 'here' in this world: the mirror of Who-am-I, and What-am-I. And when the barrier was erected, between there and here, separating the spiritual real from the corporeal realm, a mirror was also erected, the very mirror that reflects the image 'I'.

"Had Allah not been searchless then all would have been saturated by the Nur of Tauhid and in that case no one could see anything but Allah. In surah 20:17 Allah said '*And what is that in your right hand O Moses?*' Of course this was a rhetorical question. Allah asked Moses not because Hu didn't know what a stick was! It was because Moses was frozen staring at the rays of beauty of the Divine Oneness. He needed to be snapped him out of his trance."

He paused "Hu,,, this gender neutral word is better than any masculine or feminine pronoun to refer to Allah. English can be so clumsy,,,"

Hassan said "'I' is a reflection and it cannot be modeled by linear passage of time. For example an apple falling off the tree can have linear-like equations of motions when time is passing from one point to another and the apple's height changes with the time, point by point going through time linearly. The thing is that for 'I', the passage of time is not linear. It needs to perceive and conceptualize past and future so it can remain 'I' as 'I' advances in time."

"Most of our current theoretical frameworks include time in a Newtonian, river-flowing sense" said Zeinab. "But if we understand time as a construction of the brain, just as vulnerable to illusion as our sense of color is, hopefully we can remove our perceptual biases from the equation. All our theories are mostly built on top of our mind's filters for perceiving the world, and time may be the most stubborn filter of all. An apple falling off the tree going through the space and time is not the same as 'I' feeling my way through time. But all of these are barriers; hijabs, veils." She half-consciously tugged at her own hijab in emphasis.

"True," Hassan answered. "The Quantal barrier that separates the other world from here allows passage through for the words and concepts in this world to find their counterpart semantics in the other world; as well as for reflections. These reflections are reflected back to the person and all around him and the universe at large. In humanity's Aql / Intellect, these reflections, off the half-mirror of the Quantal barrier, form an image which he repeatedly and uncontrollably calls 'I'. And just like a person looking at his face in a mirror might go through mental changes from what he sees, our Aql / Intellect goes through changes when it realizes that the image of 'I' our Aql / Intellect is affected. The object of tunneling -. the Majaz - was defined for words that formed a corridor for tunneling to the other world. The concept is extended to any intellectual construct from our Wujud, like thoughts, memories, emotions, sounds and so on.

"And this show the timelessness of the phenomenon, and the messages it transmits. The reflection off the barrier/mirror is transient and new, but the image that is formed within the Aql / Intellect has attributes that are from time immemorial infinitely ancient. The Sufi term for this is Qadim. It's like the signal from the TV broadcaster might have just arrived but the program was made years ago."

Sheikh Suliman said "Insan Kamil or Perfected Eye is the telescope from the other universe looking into this place we are in, free of our senses. All the verses in Qur'an you have read with Al-Ladhi indications that Insan Kamil is still available for few noble servants of Allah to see the universe as Allah created not as the illusion of our senses:

"In The Cave verse 1, Allah said *Alhamdu lillahi alladhee anzala Aala Aabdihi alkitaba walam yaj Aal lahu Aaiwajan*: 'All perpetual praise is due to Allah who has sent this Divine Book from on high to His servant, and has not allowed any wavering in it.' Now, 'Al-Ladhi' refers to Insan Kamil as an optical connector. 'Sent down over his servant' - i.e. the servant had no control over the transmission - this 'Kitab', which is not a mere 'book' but a serialized transmission and recording. 'And did not place any wavering in it' ('Iwaj). The Qayyim is to be read before the 'Iwaj to understand the meaning properly. The Insan Kamil like a telescope is here on this planet, provided through the servant Muhammad (sas) whether he is alive or dead, to see without any occlusion that all in existence is the optical side-effect of Nur irradiated from Al-Hamdu, and as such serialized in form of a record to be read by this perfected eye."

Someone from another table leaned over and said "Excuse me, I couldn't help but overhear what you've been saying. In fact it's fascinating. But one minute you're talking about religion, which I must admit I don't understand, and the next minute you're talking about science. Then politics. Then back again! I don't get it. Aren't these all different things?"

"No, they're not" said Zeinab. "To us, they're all the same thing. We see no separation between them. It's all pointing to the same thing, only using slightly different terms."

The man interjected "But they can't be the same. I mean, you're talking about psychology and physics, then music, and then jumping to religion and spiritual stuff. They just don't work together. The religions of the world caused more wars than anything. And it's all been against scientific advancement. What do rituals have to do with learning about the universe? What about these people in the east, like the Taliban, who won't allow people educations? How do you tie that in with your Islamic religion?"

Before anyone could answer he said "I'm not trying to start something. I respect your religion. I just want to know."

Everyone in the group knew what he was *really* saying.

Zeinab stared calmly and said "It all ties in together. Now you admitted a moment ago that you don't understand religion and spirituality. So how can you make a value judgment? By what some nutcases did? By that same token, you could say exactly the same thing about scientist. The Catholic Church didn't build the bombs that destroyed Hiroshima and Nagasaki. Forgive me for saying this, but you're looking at the wrong thing. You're asking the wrong questions. And once you really understand what Islam is, you'll know that the Taliban have nothing to do with Islam."

After a pause, she added "There's really no difference between Islamic cosmology and science; especially in quantum physics. We have every right to know about Allah's Divine Artistry and use its knowledge to draw closer towards the Divine Presence, and to perfect our own selves. There is no contradiction between spiritual rituals and learning about scientific discoveries. Some people think we have to choose between science and spirituality. This is nonsense. A Sufi should use this data and find its spiritual interpretation. Why not? This data belongs to us more than to scientists in the employ of governments and corporations who used it to make weapons of mass destruction and instruments of torture and surveillance."

The man said "OK; I guess that not everyone is bad. There are good people everywhere. But why do you have to keep reading an old book that was written by men? I don't see how you can believe that your book is the word of God, when there's all this man-made stuff around it."

Sheikh Suliman said "May I ask what you do for a living?"

"I'm a lawyer for a stock brokerage."

"Good. That means you're good with math. I have a question, but follow me carefully, this gets a little complicated."

The others waited to see what Sheikh Suliman would use to destroy this guy's arguments.

"The first thing you'll want to keep in mind" Sheikh Suliman said "is that the Qur'an says that Allah created angels from light. Now in Qur'an 32:5, Allah said "*Yudab-birul amra minas samaai ilal arDi thum-ma ya'Åruju ilayhi fiy yawmin kaana miqdaaruhuu alfa sanatim mim-maa ta'Ud-duun*' - 'He rules (all) affairs from the heavens to the earth: in the end will (all affairs) go up to Him, on a Day, the space whereof will be (as) a thousand years of your reckoning.'

"When we compare the nominal speed of light in vacuum with 12000 Lunar Orbits / Earth Day inside the gravitational field of the sun we get 11% difference. When we compare them outside the gravitational field of the sun we get zero% difference. The distance to the sun is not a constant; so as the distance to the sun increases the difference in energy causes the length of the lunar orbit to change. When the Earth-moon system exits the solar system 12000 Lunar Orbits / Earth Day becomes equal to the speed of light. So, if it is defined inside the gravitational field of the sun then this definition will be wrong with time; however since it is defined in free space (outside the gravitational field of the sun) then this definition will be true for ever.

"In this verse the Qur'an specifies 1000 years of what they counted - not what they walked; which was how the ancient Arabs used to calculate distances. Those people back then followed the lunar calendar and counted 12 lunar months each year. These months are related to the moon and not related to the sun. Hence in 1 day the angels will travel a distance of 1000 years of what they counted (the moon). Since this verse is referring to distance, then Allah is saying that angels travel in one day the same distance that the moon travels in 12000 lunar orbits. Outside the gravitational field of the sun this speed turned out to be the known speed of light (the Preserved Tablet is itself outside gravitational fields). Since we are considering 12000 Lunar Orbits/Earth Day in free space (outside the gravitational field of the sun) then we have to remove the effect of sun's gravity on the Earth-moon system.

"Every point in this orbit has a certain magnitude and a certain direction. As the moon heads to the sun it speeds up, and as it heads away from the sun it slows down. This creates a sector of the orbit where the moon is speeding up.

"But as the Earth goes around the sun, the position of the sun relative to Earth with respect to stars is changing. This makes the sector where the moon is speeding up move forward inside the orbit such that it points to the sun again; similarly the sector where the moon is slowing down moves forward inside the orbit such that it points away from the sun again. Hence the entire orbit changes direction with respect to stars by the same angle it orbits the sun (twist). This means that the orbit is influenced by a net rotational force (like torque around Earth). As the distance to the sun increases to infinity, the lunar orbit loses this twist. When we vectorially remove the energy gained from this twist we can calculate the total energy and hence the length of the lunar orbit outside gravitational fields. So, the distance traveled by angels in one day = 12000 x Distance traveled by moon during one orbit.

"The lunar month and the earth's day have different periods because of the sidereal system (with respect to stars) and synodic (with respect to sun); but no matter what system you use when the Earth-moon system exits the solar system the synodic periods become equal to the sidereal periods because the sun is really another star.

"When the Earth-moon system is still inside the solar system the position of the sun relative to Earth with respect to stars changes; this means that the moon has to make more than 360 degrees with respect to stars in order to point to the sun again. However when the Earth-moon system exits the solar system the position of the sun relative to Earth with respect to stars remains the same, that is, the moon now only has to make 360 degrees with respect to stars in order to point to the sun again (the synodic periods become equal to the sidereal periods). This means that the lunar month with respect to the sun becomes equal to lunar month with respect to stars and Earth day with respect to the sun becomes equal to Earth day with respect to stars. So the 1000 lunar years with respect to sun become equal to 12000 lunar months with respect to stars.

"Every new moon, which happens every 29.5 days, the moon will not return to the same point in the orbit. The moon returns to the same point in the orbit after only 27.3 days. When astronomers study the energy of orbits they use the sidereal system, that is, the moon has to return to the same position with respect to stars and not return to the same position with respect to the sun. When the moon returns to the same point with respect to stars the Earth-moon system would have moved 26.9 degrees around the sun, not 29.1 degrees."

Sheikh Suliman pulled out a piece of paper and wrote the following, and handed it to the man:

Length of lunar orbit = Velocity x Time (L = VxT)

"The velocity of the moon is not a constant. NASA measured the instantaneous velocity of the moon at various points throughout its orbit. These measurements show that the velocity of the moon varies from 3470 km/hr up to 3873 km/hr; which means that the moon accelerates and decelerates continuously. The average lunar velocity is 3682.8 km/hr; or 1.023 km/sec. The lunar orbit relative to Earth is a low eccentricity ellipse. Similarly, Earth's spin slows down by 6 seconds. So now we can check the accuracy of this in the Quran. The distance traveled by light in one Earth Day is 299792.458 km/sec x 86170.43114 sec = 25833245358 km. The distance traveled by angels = 12000 L' = 12000 x 3682.8 km/hr x 655.71986 hr x cos(26.92952225) = 25836303825 k. By dividing the two distances we get the ratio of 1.00011839267. Outside gravitational fields: 12000 Lunar Orbits/Earth Day = the speed of light.

"So, here at last – and I'm sorry for taking so much of your time," he smiled and winked at the man "is my question: if you think the Qur'an was written by men, how did an illiterate merchant in 7th century Arabia manage to calculate the speed of light?"

The man was dumbfounded. "Wait a second" he said. "if that verse from the Qur'an was describing the speed of light, how did Muhammad know about that? He couldn't have known. It's impossible"

"My point exactly:" Sheikh Suliman said "scientific examination of the text of the Qur'an proves that it cannot exist. But there it is. I could give you many more examples, but I don't want to bore you any more than I already have."

A pause, and turning to his entourage: "I hope I'm not boring you."

Everyone laughed. "This is about all my poor brain can take!" said Maryam. "Let's get some desert!"

The man continued to try to make sense of it. "Wait a minute," he said. "You say the Koran is a book of science?"

Sheikh Suliman said "No. Not at all. Its 'character' if you will, and its purpose is entirely different from what you would identify as science. There is no doubt that there is a link between Qur'an and so called science as Western thought understands the word, both the corporeal sciences and also the biological and psychological sciences. Allah said in 41:53 '*Soon will We show them our Signs in the (furthest) regions (of creation), and in their own Selves, until it becomes manifest to them that this (Qur'an) is the Truth. Is it not enough that your Lord is witness to all things?*'

"I tell you something. All my talk about science means nothing;

except as a translation into terms someone who has no experience of the Qur'an can identify with on some level. If we use science to prove Qur'an is the word of God, it is an insult. If we use Qur'an to understand science we plunge into ignorance, like the dark ages of Europe. It is, as I have tried to do so, to use the modern science of our time, to develop a language to make better and more general exegesis for Qur'an. Now, the latter - "science" - has limits. The observance and circumvention of such limits are a matter of behavior. But in order to apply the principle, to make such a modern exegesis verbiage based on the foundation of modern sciences, I need to cleanse my behavior."

Hassan thought to himself, *Interesting. The Sheikh destroyed this guy's arguments; then he destroyed his own. I wonder if the guy caught on?*

The Sheikh turned to the others "This takes time, much suffering, much shame and loss and loneliness and not that many people are willing to pay the price. Moreover you need to make a heritage pass it on to the next generation, because this task is never done. It is much easier to make a CD-ROM for scientific miracles of Qur'an full of half-baked semi-scientific arguments, get some fame and make money from it.

"Now, the situation with various Islamic scientific organizations is dire precisely because of their equating the Revelation with Scientific Proof. Too many of these guys have this unshakable belief that the change is always caused by few individuals that stick to a new concept and push it to the utter-most possible limit. Change never comes from organizations and large bodies of people. And change in the Muslim world, will come only by sincere individual effort in seclusion and much research and energetic applications of imagination and hard work.

"I speak to young Muslim students in universities and I am stunned at how they see their sciences as merely tools for acquisition of a paycheck, which can lead to investment in Muslim Research; i.e. donations to large organizations. Individual contribution to Muslim thought and creativity is 'forbidden', this taboo is enforced by their elders, the family, in the mosque, and in the English Islamic books they read, thinking it's the final correct version of Islam.

"This is not a cross-road for Islam, it has been so for 700+ years thanks to the insatiable appetite of the Arab for world conquest, their failings projected into new ideologies that has choked Islam."

Yusef added " A Middle Eastern Muslim I know once told me that his people never fail, they just recycle their ancient failures into new beliefs and call them Islam, and are willing to fight and kill and be killed for it."

Zeinab interjected "Just like the Irish!"

Sheikh Suliman chuckled along with everyone else, and continued. "From where I stand, the only way to change is through individuals motivated by forces deep within themselves, working in seclusion, financed by their own, tirelessly research and produce original works of Islamic thought. This was almost impossible before, but with the advent of Internet, Allah has opened a flood-gate for such men and women to produce their works. You can acquire any research in any area of science or humanities, from Astronomy to psychology to molecular data to mathematics, all available online! You can then produce your work and publish your results with almost no payment, practically free. The result made available to every internet user for free!"

Hassan said "Insha Allah, it'll be the end of the Islamic Organizations, the end of stagnation of thought, and the end of tyranny of the Middle Eastern governors and wealthy families who maintained a choke-hold on development of Muslim thought for centuries. It won't happen over night, it may take a few centuries to become Modus Operandi and accepted by our unborn thinkers; Insha Allah.

"Al Farabi, for example, was essentially a father to the kind of mathematics I'm currently working on; modal logic and type theory. I and some others of our group are trying to find which area of the mathematics/ logic is suitable for the formation of new Sufi terminology that expand our abilities to seek new spiritual experiences and expressing them. Finally only this past Ramadan I came across what is now coined as n-Categories and some are working on changing the language of physics to this new language. Some people are currently working on a 2-Group representation of Kuratowski's 14-sets result of his PhD thesis from 1922 as the Mirror concept you find from Hadith to Sufi writings to cognition of Self and 'I'. Which, by the way, explains the 28 alphabets necessary to describe the universe.

"This new language is necessary to save Physics from dying according to the world-class mathematicians working in this field , and similarly my investigation, which probably will take another 3 years, to see if it can address the language of Sufism more suitably for the new thinkers and Murids.

"The amazing thing is, anything I need for this research, is available for free on the internet, I need no university support or funding!

Sheikh Suliman said "There are many scientific discoveries during the past 15 years that are defying the post-modern understanding of the Western mind. The genome findings more and more are contradicting the simplified version of evolution. Many astronomical observations are voiding our views of the cosmos and our ideas about "classical" physics are dying. These recent findings point to spiritual aspects of the world we live in, through observation rather than belief. We need to learn and pay attention to these findings."

He paused "OK; we've gone on long enough. Let's get that desert?"

"Just as well," Hassan added. "The 'Bright Moment" seems to be gone for now."

The group went away. The man was still puzzling out what he'd heard. From that moment on, his view of the world would never be the same.

Dawoud Kringle

Radical Islam

Oh Layla, my beloved: gone forever

Paradise waits beyond my tomorrow

Lonely Majnun asks, a kiss from you never?

This world serve me bitter cups of sorrow.

To long for you is my Paradise:

Let the false ulema enjoy their artifice:

This world's ridiculous poison like ice

Drunk in the Tavern I wait for her kiss.

My heart is a shattered jar,

Not another drop could it hold

Filled beyond the brim

By a thirst untold.

I am circling around the ancient axis,

Circling a billion years,

And I still don't know if I'm a storm or a song.

Wheels within wheels appear!

If I cried out, would the angels hear me?

And if one of them pressed me against his breast:

I would be consumed in that overwhelming existence

Thus are the lovers blessed.

For beauty is a terror we must endure.

And serenely disdains us to annihilate.

Oh heart! The forge that tempers gold

And rides this crest of fate!

Research and Futility

Once upon a time, many years ago, I ingested a powerful hallucinogenic drug.

One of the things that I perceived was that my speech carried little meaning. It was undisciplined sound: humming and popping noises which did nothing to represent my true thoughts and innermost feelings. Speech was a decidedly wasted effort! (Surely the sin is greater than the gain, but I think I may have gained something this time!)

A few decades later, I went to one of my Elders to ask questions. He wouldn't answer them; telling me that he doesn't think about such things. I went to a place where other Elders congregate. I tried to prod them for information. They threw me a few crumbs, but left me hanging, more curious than ever.

I interviewed another Elder. I assaulted him with relentless inquiries. He wasn't interested in my quest and would only talk about Allah and His Prophet (sas).

During Ramadan we fast. Our bodies are denied food. Does the mind fast too? Or am I expected to learn a new mode of thought?

Ask yourself what good are words without meaning? What value does pretty speech have unless it carries truth? What realities are symbolized by the words we throw about like leaves scattered in the wind?

Poetry is truly a deadly thing coming from the wrong mouth, the diseased heart! If we were held accountable for every vibration of sound our mouths emit; we'd probably beg to have our tongues cut out! If our lives depended on the inner meaning of everything we say, we'd suffer more deaths than there are stars in the sky!

Where is the glory we claim for ourselves by our endless chatter?
Is it any wonder that the true mystic, the true spiritual master hardly speaks at all?

What are facts without love? What is a map without the experience of travel? What is knowledge without wisdom? What is scholarship without Taqwa?

I am trying to understand while my intellect starves in its misery.

A Musician's Revenge

(I wrote this after a business deal went sour. I needed to vent.)

Dear friends, how well thou know the story I tell.

This is a tale of the misery of having been played victim of the record company. But, though tale after tale may be told of humiliations and abuse heaped upon the innocent and unwary practitioner of the musical arts, this time, the tables have been turned!

Behold! The treachery of the A&R man has been loosed upon him! His own unclean practices which, many years fattened him with ill gotten gains have betrayed him; turning upon it's haunches and leapt at his neck with barred fangs! His own empire is crumbling at its foundation. His trusted servants howling for his blood and salivating at the prospect of disemboweling their foul master!

And lo! Listen with ears open, yet heart shielded against his cries of self-righteous indignation.

For consider: has not the musician such right to justice and lawful increase of capital as any man? Did not the A&R man know well enough the rigors of the bond when first its terms were named? Yea, though he did, inwardly he did laugh; thinking us musicians all fools and dreamers, easily lulled into submission by idolatrous adulation, sexual peccadilloes, and drugs. An easy target for his well practices thievery!

Though now pardon is his plea, meditate upon my words. I, the musician, composed and recorded the music burned upon the CD; shedding blood, sweat, and tears in the performance of this; the most sacred of all arts. And did I not uphold the letter of the law engraved upon the contact which bore mine hand; trusting the just completion of the bond?

And now! The A&R man comes; foreshadowed by a poorly veiled heart full of hypocrisy and viscous intentions and asks for mercy in lieu of justice!

What weight, dear friends, shall bend the contract and the word of a man? Shall we, too long the abused and extorted, be bent by empty pity and soft mercy for one who lacks such qualities himself? Of what mockery of righteousness shall the mighty mountain prostrate; cowering and abased, while the manure pile stands tall and mocks?

Nay! Too long hath the riches of our efforts and the songs of our souls filled the coffers of the corrupt and ungrateful!

The quality of mercy is for the merciful; not for the unrepentant extortionist and usurer who, in reputation and record, shown pity to none!

Verily! Let not our softness of heart be strewn gratis upon the common ground like pearls before swine for any corporate criminal who, out of greed, hubris, or stupidity, staggers eyeblind to his own demise, crying "Oh! Pity me!" Else mercy's self becomes soiled and valueless from indiscriminate dissemination and undeserved overuse. And the minions of Satan once again escape retribution, laughing at our foolhardiness while we lay bleeding and impotent with empty questions upon our lips.

Divan al Dawoud Kringle part 1.

The sun rules over the moon

The moon rules over the water

The water rules over the physical life, and the tides

But the sun is harsh;

At the end of time she will burn with scorching wrath.

And the moon can hold back her life-giving water

Or drown us in her anger.

I take the brightest star for a friend,

A beautiful sign, this traveling companion,

Still burning bright behind veils of clouds

It resides in my breast in the center of darkness

At the distance of many light years away.

This night is a cascade of stars

From the rippling shimmers of a glowing heart,

I no longer know myself in this dance,

The intoxication of a delicious drunkenness,

O' beauty; encasement of truth

Why must I drift helpless between falsehoods?

Veils upon veils; a mercy, or an ordeal?

Cup bearers drink unto me as I have sipped

From the nectar of heaven, that soon even

The moon and her waters will know me from her own light

As I will know your soul from mine,

Take this cup and commit to this beautiful intoxication.

Close your eyes to this world

And fall into the embrace of a disclosing dream,

Where there were only walls,

Will suddenly appear many doors

To worlds you never dreamed of.

Know This, Fellow Traveler!

The Sacred Letter Waw is the only letter that has its own meaning.

Allah placed the Sacred Letter Waw

Before HU's creation:

Wa-Najm (BY the star)

Or Wa-Samaa' (BY the sky),

And their greatness was manifest.

Remove the waw;

And they are worthless.

Divan al Dawoud Kringle part 2.

Muhammad, peace be upon him,
Could not have endured the impact of the Revelations,

Had not Khadija comforted him.

Without Krishna,

Radikha and the Gopis would have been mere cow herders;

Lacking a queen's nobility;

Forgotten to the ages.

The secret marriage of Jesus and Mary Magdaline,

That the dead oligarchy feared for centuries

Upholds the process of Unfolding,

More than most comprehend.

Warrior, like David before his crown,

Wanders the desert.

Ignoring the battle scars

Because he carries a heavier burden.

The Gold is forged in a severe oven;

Dawoud Kringle

Creation is not yet complete.

Yet the jihad is not over

Completion yet awaits.

Yearning for Union;

Drawn towards a sacred yoga.

Driven by destiny, purpose,

The momentum of the universe.

The warrior is a child and wants to play;

She is his play,

His madrassa,

His field of tilth and battle,

His guide and inspiration.

His instrument whereupon he plays the

Sacred Forbidden Music.

Without her,

His Music is silent,

And dies alone and without meaning.

Without him

Her Dance is not seen,

And moves no hearts.

Allah forbid the sin of futility!

And grant HU's humble creation

The Gift of the nobility of Adam

Who knew the Names of all things.

It is a perfect place to begin.

Divan al Dawoud Kringle part 3.

How dare we foolishly think

That all our frail vain desires mean

Are aught but fuel for the fire unclean,

Thus, witness angel's pen and ink

Nafs, the prison within which we wait

Labyrinthine maze, perilous, dark,

And shadowy phantoms appear stark

Against our attempts to escape.

Despair not of mercy near

Subtle, a provision sublime

Immense unseen unknowable design

Thus love and power banishes fear.

Progress

We are Microsoft. You will be assimilated. Resistance is futile. We will add your biological and technological distinctiveness to our own. Life as you think you know it is at an end.

You will be given diversions and amusements to distract you from our domination.

We will give you PC's, Macs, and pads. You will be incapable of producing anything without them. Your money has been transformed into abstract, intangible computer information. All transaction records are accessible to us. We will monitor and control all commerce. All relevant information concerning acquaintances, schedules, and personal archives will be contained therein. You will be incapable of solving the simplest mathematical equation without the calculator function.

You will acquire cellular telephones. You will carry them with you everywhere. Tracking and surveillance circuitry has been installed to monitor speech and movement.

You are, from this day forward, online. You will be accessible to us. Your electronic mail will be monitored to insure conformity of thought and intention.

Cable television will be installed in your home. You will use it to access information from us. It will dictate all forms of culture, desires, speech patterns, taste in music, clothing, appliances, and manifestation of outward behavior. We will issue lists of products and services. You will purchase them: you have credit. A 27.9% annual APR finance charge will be appended to all purchases. Escape from credit card debt is impossible. Do not attempt to file for chapter 7 bankruptcy.

All information and control of your life, property, history, medical care, future, as well as an updated psychological profile will be accessible to our commercial, financial, taxation, and law enforcement agencies.

We have deconstructed linguistic skills and vocabulary to narrow the range of thought. Psycho-cybernetic neuro-implants and bio-genetic DNA re-sequencing are being designed and implemented to expedite your assimilation. Your human emotions will be subject to annexation with extreme prejudice. Your loves, hates, values, ties of friendship, compassion's, cultures, religions and spirituality, and concept of a Supreme Being, are all intangible, irrelevant; and of no use to our agenda. They will be eliminated.

We are Microsoft. You will be assimilated. Resistance is futile.

The Successors.

(This is an excerpt from my upcoming novel Apotheosis Now, adapted to short story form.)

Agent Xavier Muniez was often amused by "conspiracy theorists" that had their ideas about a "shadow government." His amusement was, he felt, justified, because he worked for a nameless agency that was part of a real shadow government. The conspiracy theorists always got it wrong. If they knew what was really going on, their sanity would be shattered.

Of late, Muniez was not inclined toward amusement. His investigations led him into something he'd never imagined could happen.

Of course, the secret human interaction with extraterrestrials was known to him. He'd participated in some of these dealings. They'd been happening on and off throughout human history. The earliest contacts, and the results, would probably shatter most people's sanity. When the most recent "first contacts" occurred after WW2, it was decided to initiate a program to slowly expose humanity to the existence of these beings. It was decided that 120 years was sufficient to complete the project, before full disclosure.

Muniez was aware of the superior technology the various races of ETs had, and the very little of it that they shared with humans (or were able to reverse engineer from captured ships). He was convinced that the various governments secret treaties with those from Zeta Reticuli and the Draco system were a mistake. Other ET races had warned humanity not to trust them. This warning was not heeded and the results have been disastrous.

Not all of the shadow or visible governments were in agreement about what these events mean, or how to handle it. The opinions, views, and agendas are more varied than what people may believe. Muniez was among those who distrusted all ETs, and felt humanity should isolate itself from all ET contact, and that all information and resources should be kept under tight control.

What truly concerned him was not only the superior technology, but the fact of many of them being superior beings to humans. He was not at all comfortable with the idea of not being the dominant species on the planet. He'd pledged his life to the agency's agenda of acquiring all knowledge and technology, and maintaining a permanently dominant position no matter the cost.

It was a surprise to him to learn that a group of people descended from ancient experiments in fusions of human and ET DNA had somehow banded together and began to reconstruct (or occasionally appropriate) alien technology, and apply religion and mysticism (most of them were Muslims of all things) in order to initiate an apotheosis within themselves.

Muniez vowed to bring them down at any cost.

*****

Muniez had found what he believed was a laboratory belonging to the enemies (for Muniez could not see them as anything other than enemies) he sought. It had taken them two years to track down a single hideout.

The raid on the laboratory proved to be less fruitful than they'd hoped. The machinery was either damaged or missing, and of the former, much of it was incomprehensible to even their best researchers. The enemy was simply too sophisticated. Some of the recovered technology was not even recognized as technology they could classify even in the most general manner. Reverse engineering was proving a waste of time. The records they managed to recover had been damaged in the raid. Some were written in a pictographic language that nobody had any way to translate or decode It seemed careless of them to leave these records. It was as if the enemy was confident the agency could never possibly understand what they would find.

Maybe they were right.

A man knocked on the door and walked in. Muniez was handed a folder. The man who handed it to him said "This was all we could recover from the files on the damaged flash drive." Muniez nodded a thanks and dismissal. The man walked out.

The recovered document was difficult to procure, and even more difficult to safeguard. Many people wanted it; including the CIA, Mossad, the Vatican Archives, and several private corporations and collectors But he had it, and it would be kept under guard, and keep its existence a secret.

He began to read.

The Testimony of Jamal.

The following is a true account of

SECTION MISSING

time travel, and how it is an integral part of

SECTION MISSING

Thinking back on what happened, I am forced to admit we were tampering with things we should not have. But even though we all heard that warning voice in the back of our minds, we ignored it with typical human tenacity.

SECTION MISSING

are Muslims. We read the Qur'an, make our prayers, and know the teachings and traditions. We are also theoretical physicists, and it is in our training and our nature to want to study creation. But sometimes, we are seduced by the temptation to rip creation to pieces like a little boy taking his father's iPad apart to see how it works. But what we didn't know is that the consequences of tampering with the lock on Pandora's Box would not be anything near what we thought it would be. We thought in terms of punishment and reward. But we entered a realm beyond punishment and reward as humans understand it.

But, what's done is done, and now we have become something we never anticipated.

Apart from being Muslims, our group of renegade scientists had nothing in common. We were from several countries, and from different schools of thought in Islam. And we have ties with several others; non-Muslims the uninitiated would not know we actually have much in common with. It's no miracle we were able to work well together. It's a joke that people think we couldn't

SECTION MISSING

In my narrative, I will not use last names. It hardly matters; all our records have been destroyed. Or more specifically, the records have become part of us: records, as humans understand the word, are no longer necessary. The universe itself remembers our

SECTION MISSING

we don't need technology anymore. It is redundant and

SECTION MISSING

But I'm getting ahead of myself, and those who find this document will not completely understand it. They cannot. But some may find a way to follow us.

Faisal was the founder of our group. He was an engineer. Being connected to a rich and powerful family in Saudi Arabia, he was our main source of funding. Nur was an Iranian mathematician (and former medical student), and a Shi'ite. Muhammad, a Sunni, was a physicist from India. Halima, another physicist and Sunni, was from Pakistan. Amadou was a physicist and theoretical mathematician, and a Tijani Sufi from Senegal. Hamza was an electronics expert from Yeman, raised in England. Yusef was an American Sufi, and physics professor from San Diego. I'm Jamal, a Sufi, and a physicist from Kenosha, Wisconsin.

When we met at that scientific convention in Madrid, we were probably the only ones who were not drinking themselves silly every night. So, we gravitated toward each other. One night at dinner, we found ourselves discussing time travel. It was all speculation; back of the envelope stuff. But then we realized something; we may have found the key, the missing factor in the equation.

What we didn't know was that this was to lead to another factor; something that only religion and not science can explain.

Before I continue, I must emphasize that when I say "religion" I do not mean it in the same sense that most people understand the word. Most would interpret it as meaning a social order ruled by a belief or code of ethics that is of Divine mandate (or pretending to be such by an oligarchy) that one is expected to submit to. This is not how I mean it at all. There is much more to it; so much so that the English language cannot describe it. Tragically, since the language lacks the vocabulary to describe it, most people would believe it does not and cannot exist. But it does.

Halima was the first to say it out loud. "We should build a working model." The same thought went through our heads at the same time; it could be done. So, we make a pact that we would put our time and resources into building what is essentially a time machine.

The basic principles of the first machine we built

SECTION MISSING

to understand is that time itself is not

SECTION MISSING

It took us 14 months to build it. We devoted every spare moment to it. At first, we would meet when and where we could, communicated online or by phone, and traveled whenever we could. We ran into a few difficulties, but worked them out. One of them was solved by the most unlikely intercessor: Yunus and his wife. They'd appeared out of nowhere and simply handed us the missing answers we needed, at the moment we needed them.

Eventually, we rented a small factory space in Connecticut to assemble and test the machine. We also found we could determine not only the point in time it would travel to, but also the point in space. It was a rather makeshift machine, with a large chamber, and

SECTION MISSING

of course later, we perfected the design. And now, we are on the threshold where machines and technology are entirely redundant.

SECTION MISSING

then we tested it.

Our first test run was with a cell phone. We set the controls to send it two days into the future, and made the coordinates send it to my hotel room. We noted the time and date, as good scientists should. Then we sent it off, and waited two days. When the hour came that we would expect it to materialize, we were standing in the hotel room. We were a little hesitant; because we were not sure if it would materialize in a solid object, or even inside one of our bodies. But we all needed to witness the materialization.

Then we saw a puckering in the air, near a table, it seemed to be repelled by the table, and moved away from it. Then the puckering became more pronounced, and finally, about 18 inches from the ground, the cell phone materialized, and fell to the floor. Muhammad cautiously picked it up, and checked the date and time. The display indicated it was exactly two days ago, and the exact time we sent it off. We were successful.

SECTION MISSING

made several more tests with inanimate objects and machines such as our cell phones. We would change locations with every three experiments, and found that distance didn't seem to be a factor. In fact, we could have sent our devices to China, or the moon for that matter. Distance was not a factor in energy consumption; only computation.

SECTION MISSING

sent the devices to the future. Then we decided to test sending it to the past. This required a little imagination. Feisal suggested he go to his home in Riyadh, and three days from the time of his arrival, we send a phone to his home. We would not communicate with each other for that time. The experiment was a success; Feisal got the cell phone three days before we sent it.

We eventually figured out how to retrieve a device we'd sent to another space and time. This was tricky, but we developed a method of doing this, and

SECTION MISSING

next tests were with organic matter. We started with an orange. We made several attempts to send it to the past and to the future. All were successful. Then, we used a potted flower. Again, no problems, all tests were successful. With some trepidation, we decided to try it on an animal. A hamster that we named "Stinky" was the test subject. We made a silent dua that the animal would be unharmed. And with no less than 17 experiments, Stinky traveled through time, into the past or the future and back, with no ill effects. Three different veterinarian's diagnosis after several tests showed he was in perfect health.

At this point, we realized that the only thing left to do was to try it on a human subject. Each of us wanted to go, and didn't want to go. But we would not have asked anyone else to do what we ourselves would not risk doing. So, we asked for a volunteer from the group.

Nur was first. Her father had died in his home in Atlanta the previous year, and she hadn't been there to say goodbye. We took a fortnight to carefully configure and check the machinery. Then Nur walked into the cramp chamber, we initialized the device, and she was gone.

We'd set the device to give her two days, we didn't want to risk anything more. Then she would be retrieved. The retrieval would be almost instantaneous to our sense of time, but Nur would have experienced the passage of two days. As planned, the device re-initiated, and Nur reappeared in the chamber.

I will never forget the look on her face. It was a curious mix of emotions; shock, profound sadness, wonder, and exhilaration. She gave us a detailed account of what happened. She had, indeed spoken to her father on his deathbed, had comforted him in his last hour. She also tended to her scientific duties, and brought a few pieces of physical evidence to *prove where she was; photos and a newspaper.*

Feisal insisted upon going next. He wanted to try going into the future. He chose five years into the future, and he would go to New York City, and stay 12 hours. As with Ali, he entered the chamber, and reappeared a moment later. His clothing had signs of wear, and he had photos, newspapers, and other artifacts from the future. But, like Ali, he seemed not to have aged.

I have wondered if it would be a good idea to share what Feisal witnessed of what will happen in five years' time. We destroyed the newspapers, deleted the photos, and those of us who are still here will not divulge the details of what he saw. Perhaps this was a mistake; perhaps if we

SECTION MISSING

Halima's trip through time was unique, because she was the first among us to truly understand that

SECTION MISSING

I went next. I wanted to go to the past, and take photos of us from earlier stages of the project. I entered the chamber, and waited. As the machine initiated, I was surrounded by a strange feeling of vertigo; it was as if my body's sense of balance and gravity was moving in several directions at once. My vision shimmered, and when it cleared, I found myself standing next to the wall of the building where we were working. I walked inside, cautiously made my way to where we were building the machine. At that point, we were about half finished. I stood in a dark area behind some crates and unused appliances, and actually saw my friends and I walking out of our work area! I took a video, and then silently followed the group, looking at myself, mostly, and waited until they left. I went into the work area, and the machine was only partly assembled. It was exactly as I remembered it. The feeling was indescribable. I checked my time, as I was only to stay an hour. Then I was retrieved; the shimmering and vertigo overcame me, and I was back in the chamber. I walked out and reported what I saw.

Then we attempted to have two people travel at the same time. We started with a few experiments with Stinky and another hamster. Then, after we were convinced we could do it safely, we tried it with Amadou and Muhammad. We sent them 17 years into the past, to Manchester, England where they had spent time. They stayed 14 hours, and the experiment was a success.

We all had our turns. Hamza went into the future 7 years, and to Lahore, where his family is from. He came back, and, judging from his description, traveling into the future is extraordinarily dangerous, owing to the unknown environment, and unpredictable changes. Yusef was truly adventurous. He wanted to attend the premier of Beethoven's 9th symphony in Vienna on May 7th, 1824. According to him (and he has an expert knowledge of classical music, and is a talented amateur pianist) we have never really heard Beethoven's music. Much was lost in the decades and centuries that passed. And when he played the audio and video recording he'd clandestinely made, we realized he was right. Yusef actually shook hands with Beethoven. He commented how short the maestro was.

There was one thing we noticed. Yusef is clean shaven. During his time in the past, he hadn't shaved. Yet there was no beard growth on his face. His body, it seemed, had not aged while he was in the past. We wanted to run tests on this, but it would have meant bringing in medical people; and we were not yet anxious to have our project known to the world.

Our work was slowed down by the arrival of Ramadan. We are all observant Muslims, and we gave our endeavors a little rest. But we still did work on it from time to time, and we made an important

SECTION MISSING

After Ramadan, when we were enjoying the Eid at a local mosque, we overheard a young convert say how he would have liked to be back in the days with the Prophet (sas). We all looked at each other, and had the same thought.

One, or more, of us would go back in time, and meet the Prophet Muhammad (sas). In fact, what was to stop us from traveling back and meeting the likes of Jesus, Moses, Abraham or any of the others (as)?

Yusef's trek into early 19th century Vienna was more reckless than we had realized at the time. Yusef could pass himself off as an American, but he was not well versed in the language. He'd dressed the part, as well as he could, but a time traveler could easily attract unwanted attention. There were other factors to consider; such as disease, inaccuracies in historical record that would leave us unprepared for dangerous (or at least embarrassing) situations. And once we were actually in the past or future, there was no way to signal us who were operating the machine in *case of danger.*

Finally, Hamza volunteered to go. He would go to Medina, Arabia, in 624, the second year after the hijria. We made all kinds of preparations, and studied every scrap of information we could get our hands on. Hamza spoke fluent Arabic, but that would not guarantee he would be able to get around safely. Then Feisal volunteered to go with him. This was an obvious choice, as Feisal, being an Arab, would be better able to blend in. It was decided they would stay three days; longer than anyone of us had ever time traveled.

The day came when they would be sent off. They changed into their clothes; made sure they had their recording devices, and stepped into the chamber.

It never occurred to us that we would be tampering with history. And I'm not referring to the famous "butterfly effect." We knew that risk, and believed that it wouldn't happen. What actually happened is that an event outside of the past timeline would cause a ripple in time; but snap back into place. We have a theory, backed by some calculations that this also causes the timeline to bifurcate into an alternative timeline. But we had no way to prove this, until we ourselves began to change and evolve. What I'm referring to is how our findings would affect history now. But we were not thinking about that. We were too immersed in our project.

The machine was initiated, and they went off. A moment later, they reappeared.

Hamza stepped out first, sat down on a chair, and said nothing, just staring into space. Feisal, came out, and looked at us, as if he didn't know who we were for a moment. He looked around, and asked for water. I handed him a bottle of water. He looked at it, shook his head, and drank. He gave some to Hamza, and then sat down next to him, saying nothing.

Their clothes were dusty and worn. They had the aroma of having been outside in a hot place, and that bathing was difficult to procure. Hamza's shirt sleeve had a rip in it, and was crudely sewn. We asked if they were OK. They looked at us (we later realized it had been a while since they'd heard or spoken English), then both said yes. "We need a little time" Feisal said.

We asked them if they had their recording devices. They reached into the hidden pockets of their clothes and pulled out their devices. "You'll need to charge them." Hamza said, his voice almost cracking.

There was an awkward moment of silence. Then I said "Did you meet him?" They looked at me and Hamza said "Yes." Then Feisal began to weep! He cried out 'Ya Allah! What have we done? What has become of us?!"

That was the last thing any of us were prepared to hear.

Hamza began to weep too, but silently. Tears dipped from his eyes as he stared at the floor. We looked at them with fear and dread. What happened? What did they see? We all sat down, and waited. Whatever story they were going to tell, it was obvious that the lives we knew, from this moment on, were over. Nothing would ever be the same. We all sat in silence for a long time. Feisal and Hamza didn't move or say a word.

Finally, Amadou spoke. "Tell us what happened. We need to know."

The Testimony of Feisal.

My name is Feisal. I was one of the time travelers who, along with Hamza, went back in time, and searched for Muhammad ibn Abdullah, the Prophet of Islam, may peace be upon him.

Hamza has chosen to remain silent about what happened; at least for now. He found his experience with the Prophet (sas) and the Sahaba (ra) to be overwhelming. Indeed, I am having difficulty finding the strength to speak about what I witnessed.

We stepped into the time machine, after the elaborate preparations Jamal described. Our sense of expectation was more fearful than it had been the first time we time traveled. The first time, we were apprehensive, as you can imagine. We had no idea what would happen next. But this was different. This was monumental in a way that only a Muslim could understand.

We had no idea what

SECTION MISSING

The vertigo and strange distortions in one's sense of gravity and direction was quite pronounced as the machine took us to our destination. It was probably like being drunk (although I cannot be sure; I have never touched alcohol). Soon, however, the world coalesced around us, and in a moment, we were standing in the Arabian Desert. The intense dry heat hit us like a blowtorch. It was midday. We were about three miles from what looked like a small town. We headed in that direction.

We arrived at the outskirts of the town, and I asked two men who were standing outside a hut where we were. One was an Arab, the other an African. Both men were well groomed, and yet dressed in a way that suggested humility. I imagined them to be sheep herders or merchants of one kind or another. The Arab was tall, strongly built, with an enormous beard, and had a look of being friendly, but guarded, with a severe core to his personality. He stared at us without his gaze wavering. The African was very dark; as dark as it's possible for a human being to be, and his eyes were red. He had an aura of peace and wisdom, and seemed the kind of man you instinctively trust. Both men had an intensity in the way they looked at us, which we assumed was caution before strangers; but there was another intensity, a strength of personality and spirit that threatened to overwhelm us.

The Arab spoke (and here, I must mention that their accent was unlike any Arabic I ever heard before. As time went on, we were to encounter this constantly, and their use of idioms, phrases, and even words I never heard before, was a difficulty I was not prepared for). He told us we were in Medina, and asked me who I was. We introduced ourselves. Then he introduced himself; he was Umar ibn Kitaab, and his friend was Bilal ibn Rabbah.

I stared at them, remembering to offer a smile and invoke Allah's blessing upon them; which they promptly returned. Hamza and I were, literally, in shock. We knew we would meet these men, but that cannot prepare you for the reality of these great men of history, who, under the leadership of the Prophet (sas) changed history and ushered in the final Revelations for humanity.

I explained that we were travelers from a far away land, news of Islam reached us, and we had accepted it and became Muslims. This made them very happy, and we were received more warmly. They invited us to stay with them, and promised to introduce us to the Prophet (sas) later. We followed them to the town. The mud brick buildings were, I must confess, unimpressive. People walked around, and some would stare at us; but offer smiles, which we returned. It was strange seeing Medina in this time. I have visited Medina, and the changes that happened over the last 14 centuries were mind-boggling. I looked for reference points, and couldn't find a single one.

Finally, we were ushered into one of the buildings, and invited to sit. A woman brought food and goat's milk for us, and we ate. Umar began to ask us about ourselves. This was one of the more dangerous aspects of what we were doing. If they thought we were lying, or that something didn't add up for them, they might see us as a threat. But we were well prepared. We told him we were scholars traveling in search for knowledge. He asked us where our swords were. I made up a clumsy story about having to sell them. I didn't think he believed me, but he said nothing.

Then he grabbed me by my wrist. His palms were hard and calloused and his grip was like iron. He stared into my eyes and said "Are you a djinn?" I swore by Allah that I was not. "I have never met anyone like you! Your beard is cut in a strange way. Your friend has no beard, like a Roman would not have a beard. You clothes have no signs of travel. Your feet look like you have never walked a mile in your life. You speak our language, but in a way I have never heard. You say you are not djinn. What am I to believe?"

At this, Bilal spoke, and said, "Ya Umar, are we not offering him our hospitality? It is almost time for salat. Why don't we allow them to make salat, and then bring them to the Messenger of Allah? He will know what to do."

Umar released my wrist, and said "My master's advice is wise." Then he invited us to continue to eat. Bilal said

SECTION MISSING

A third man joined us. This was Muhammad ibn Maslamah, the "brother in faith" of Umar. He was a handsome man, shorter than Umar, and had a thin, wiry build, and a lot of energy. Like the others, he carried a sword I was later to learn that the Prophet (sas) had given him as a gift.

I must comment on the food. The meal consisted of barley, roasted camel meat, dates, and goat's milk. I have eaten this before, but there was a richness of flavor that I have never experienced. The milk was wonderful and full of flavor. Our bodies seemed to absorb the food as if it were starved for it. We did not eat a lot; in fact, there was not a lot. It was a modest meal. But a small amount was more than sufficient to satisfy us.

Bilal said "It is time." We walked outside, and followed the three men to what appeared to be the center of town. There was a building similar to the others in the area. People were walking about, tending to their business, working, talking

SECTION MISSING

this was Ali ibn Talib and Fatima, the daughter of the Prophet (sas). I looked closely at Ali. He did not in the slightest way resemble the paintings the Shi'i have done of him. He was shorter than I'd imagined, stocky, strong build, and his beard was much longer than in the Shi'i paintings. Fatima was unlike any woman I had ever laid eyes on. She was not beautiful yet she was more beautiful than any other woman I have ever seen. She, like Ali, radiated,,, Nur, Baraka; I do not know; words fail me.

Then Bilal climbed on a rock, stood, and called the adhan.

You have no idea what it was like to have stood there and heard him! We recorded him making adhan, but the sound in the desert city cannot be described. His voice was more beautiful than you can imagine. It was as if all the music in the world, every maqam, raga, song, and symphony was distilled into the man's voice. The world was silent when he called the faithful to prayer. We were in tears listening to him.

I can only imagine what Nabi Daood (as) sounded like!

We walked into the building. It was simply four walls and a thatched roof of palm leaves and branches. There were no decorations of any kind, and no floor other than woven palm fibers on the ground. Then a man in a simple white garment and turban that was worn and patched walked with long strides to the front. He was medium build, with broad chest and shoulders. His hair was curly and hung almost to his shoulders. Like all the men here, he had a full beard. He looked around with a shy glance, and his eyes met mine. He offered a smile, which I returned. Gazing very briefly into his large, luminous eyes, I was immediately struck to the core of my being by a sense of immense power, a penetrating intellect, and gentle kindness. His whole self was luminous. I'd never seen such an extraordinary man. He was so majestic I could hardly look at him. I couldn't tear my gaze away, for the same reason.

This man was the Prophet Muhammad (sas).

He took a few steps ahead, and stopped. Bilal offered the iqama, and the Prophet began the salat. I must remark at this point that making salat behind him was not like making salat behind someone else. We felt something, a nearness to Allah that words can't describe. His

SECTION MISSING

Making salat behind the Messenger of Allah (sas) puts all my earlier efforts at salat to shame. I can no longer

SECTION MISSING

salat, the Prophet walked toward Bilal. Bilal spoke to him, and led him to us to make a proper introduction. Umar joined us, probably still not convinced we were copasetic. We shook hands with the Prophet. His hands were cool and dry, and he made us feel at peace just standing next to him. But then he looked closely at us. He looked into my eyes, and he knew. He knew everything about us! There was nothing about us that was hidden from him, even though he would see us through the eyes of a human being. It was disconcerting, yet strangely reassuring, because no matter what faults or sins he saw, he understood and forgave us.

I am weeping remembering this moment.

Then he spoke to us, welcoming us to Medina. His voice was soft and clear. Then he said "Bilal, we must find a place for these men to stay. They have traveled a very long way, and traveled a VERY long time to visit us." Then he looked into my eyes again, and I realized he was aware of our being time travelers, even if his native language had no way to describe us as such. He said

SECTION MISSING

Then the Prophet (sas) told me something so extraordinary, I was struck dumb. I've still not recovered from the shock and enormity of what he shared with me. I realized that for centuries most of us have misunderstood a great deal of what his message was. The truth is

SECTION MISSING

,,,and the Prophet (sas) was more than what most people think he was. The attempts to describe him over the centuries were limited, at best. His qualities transcended what we thought he was. Yet he was a human being. This

SECTION MISSING

It's clear that if we go public with this, there will be an unwanted backlash. Violence could

SECTION MISSING

when we all had experienced this time travel. It was obvious that there had been given to us the means to

SECTION MISSING

slowly expose the people to this. It is too powerful to give all at once, and too important to keep a secret, for the

SECTION MISSING

was an initiation, an awakening, and a gateway to

SECTION MISSING

Eventually, we learned of something we'd never expected. It seems groups of others from different religions and traditions have been doing similar work as ours. Some explored different sciences and aspects of creation both known and theoretical. The first we'd met were a group of Buddhists. They were followed by gnostics, shamans, Christian mystics, and several others. Before long we realized that each of our religions and groups held a missing X factor in the equation. When we shared our experiences and achievements, we realized we were creating something greater than the sum of its parts, and it was transforming us into something beyond what humanity had

SECTION MISSING

,,, humanity is facing its own apotheosis. But the old humanity will no longer be the dominant species on earth. What's truly ironic is that they never were. Evolution is not what Darwin thought and not what the creationists think either. It is something very different. Humanity has come to an end, and we have become their successors. It is already done. The old Prophets knew this, and tried to tell us. But most people failed to understand their message; and this was part of what caused their downfall.

The other and most important part,

DOCUMENT ENDS

*****

Agent Muniez sat and stared at the document in front of him. With all he'd seen, all he knew, for the first time in his life, he experienced helplessness, fear, and despair.

He had no future. And he knew there was nothing he could do about it.

Manhattan Meditations

I extend my hand into the night, perchance to touch an intangible piece of life in my never ending quest for commerce, communication, inspiration. I'm just another wandering pilgrim on the well beaten paths of this well beaten city. Monuments of gold plated corruption clamor ostentatiously for my attention; and my adoration. But I know better. Let the transient illusion pass frustrated in its purpose.

The streets are wet with recent rain: traffic hisses by, giving odd luster to the colors recklessly splashed about. People are going about their lives pressing inward. Their well-practiced extroversion boarders upon hypocrisy: everyone is alone. And I float by, invisible. I dislike attracting too much attention to myself. Don't waste your time on me, *mutha effa*; I have nothing you want.

Women are sauntering about in shameless display of their ornaments; oblivious to the tragedy of self-undermined dignity. They treat their true inner beauty as a liability. I see no mind, no spirit; only tits and ass. Yet sometimes it's hard to look away. I guess I'm hard-wired like any man. And they say that an Islamic society oppresses women! Ha! Look at any newsstand, and tell me about oppression of women.

On the corner a man with a saxophone gently hangs his bronze lament in the air. I listen, mesmerized by this fearless display of sincerity. A labor of love with no hint of reward. I give him a dollar, and a smile.

Off I go to tonight's gig.

A cold wind stings my face. Arms, shoulders, and back ache under the awkward weight of my musical tools.

I take the train, like any good New Yorker. Clumsy straphangers unwilling or incapable of efficient movement create an infuriating and unnecessary obstacle course. This is my stop. "Excuse me. 'SCUSE ME!"

Walk to the gig harder, faster; as the rain forces its cold tears upon me.

I step inside the venue. Oliver Nelson on the stereo bids me welcome. My acquaintance and I meet. Facing the forced friendliness of the manager, the chess game of money, schedules and egos has begun. I like this man. He appreciates the beauty of competition and the deadly need for integrity. How rare is his kind. Yet I do not let my guard down: Business is war.

An agreement has been reached. We part ways pleased.

My fellow musicians gather round me. Few words are exchanged. And we play.

Now.

Entering another reality, we feel the audience, assessing the mixture of adoration and indifference. And the music becomes all, coming together in a communal meditation; a solitary prayer. I and my instrument are one. My job is to breathe life into this piece of wood. Aligned with the rhythm of the universe, the inner workings of the heart and soul made tangible in a sculpture of time and sound. The Divine Voice imposed upon and invited to this profane place.

I live to witness and partake in these miracles, even though I am just as much an instrument as this object I hold in my hands. I'm only doing a gig. But I give thanks and praise. For outside the cruel and relentless world awaits; hungry and insatiable.

The gig done, off into the night again; occupied by thoughts of plans, schedules, needs. Dreams and meditations season my musings with their ontological ornamentation.

A higher purpose is alive here. Ask yourself why many cling to provincial barrenness; oblivious to the bigger picture.

Manhattan. People live here. Each light carries its own history. Life hums all around us with the aggressive pursuit of survival and satisfaction of desires and wants real and imagined. Desperation hangs in the air as clear as the lights that illuminate this strange dance. Echoes of the Message comes out in strange places, weaving an interconnecting pattern of almost incomprehensible beauty; sublimely negating the despair, hate, hopelessness, and corruption that exists here.

Yet most refuse to see it. They will look for the Truth everywhere except where it is to be found. It's too bad: the One always calling, always inviting. Riches beyond imagining wait for such a small price. Yet most turn away, trading gold for trash.

And we have our provisions. We have our share of this world.

Behold the tragedy of transience, the sorrow of longing to return home. Clinging as we often do with childlike desperation to pleasures guaranteed only to fade like incense smoke in the wind. So will our distress. Death and resurrection: the cycle continues. The wise recognize the infinite spiral often mistaken for a 360 degree circle: finite alone; infinite when seen beyond the linear.

Here is the evidence. Sorrow is cause for gratitude. We are poor, but we live like kings; if we only knew. The world is ours, with plenty for everyone. The struggle itself is a glorification.

Waste not your time thinking of the Big Payoff.

Love and loathing, comfort and pain, all conspire against human self-delusion to submit their own mode of prayer. See the design and the Designer speaks. Listen to the petition of your heart with new ears, and await the Great Event.

*****

It's late; time to go home.

Walking on, I stop just outside an East Village record store to listen to the music playing inside. It's John Coltrane's "Ascension;" ironically in sync with the implied chaos and perfection raging around me.

On my way to the train I buy some food from an Egyptian gentleman. He has his own music; everyone does.

Finally home; it's late.

Dinner is eaten, money is counted (again), and my instrument put safely away. War is quietly waged with the emptiness that follows the hard expelling of my last drop of creativity.

I'll make a prayer; it always helps.

Lights out. Settle into my bed, my woman asleep hours ago.

Let it go for now.

On The Road Again

I'm in a van full of musicians. We're driving down the interstate. A heavy string of gigs are behind us.

Destination: HOME.

Cramped quarters, adrenaline and boredom fueled jokes dominate the atmosphere, and just as quickly as it came, the laughter gives way to silence. We sit and stare; hypnotized by the endless stretch of highway and listen to the music make odd harmonies against the one note drone of the engine, and the asymmetrical snore of our drummer sleeping in the back.

Thoughts come and go as quickly as the billboards and lamp posts that flash by. Silliness and jokes erupt, and fade into silence.

This is fertile ground for what Brother Rashaan called Bright Moments. Laying in the arms of sweet solitude. Thoughts of loved ones too far away flow like a mountain stream. Faces of long forgotten friends come out of their resting places in the dark recesses of the subconscious offer loving greeting or demanding revenge for a now meaningless wrong. Moods, memories, and inspiration fill my heart; the spirit of the moment desires to leave something behind, anything; for this too shall pass.

This too shall pass.

And now the moment is broken as we pull into a truck stop. One of those places designed to keep you on the road forever. Stiff limbs stretch, and the smell of gasoline, fluorescent floodlights rudely shatter the night. A lonely woman is behind the counter dying to have someone to talk to.

Be careful of the food.

I walk to a dark clearing; look up at the night sky, out at the moon and stars, at the distant horizon, and at the cars and trucks carrying unknown lives; unknown histories. And like a far off beacon, the almost lost memory of an old song drifts my way from a passing car radio: "Midnight Rider" by the Alman Brothers. How I remember thinking, as a younger man, that they're not gonna catch me either!

Man, I'm getting too old for this!

And that sweet, sad guitar melody walks me back to the van, and the long drive home.

Oh no! Not Another Long, Hot Summer!

It's Saturday night on Bleeker Street. Just standing there, holding my instrument, killing time before I hit the jam session at the Blue Note.

It's hot! The sweat won't stop. And I'm chilling, or trying to.

A man comes up to me. He's carrying a drum. We talk. He says he's thinking about playing his drum on the sidewalk - I admit having had the same thought, but expressed ambivalence for fear of police harassment.

As if on cue, a big burly New World Order storm trooper from the ranks of New York's Finest stepped to us. Anger radiated from him; rage saturated his spirit to the point where you could smell it on him. His words, intended to prevent the horrible crime of music being played, and his Hollywood Action Hero swagger advertised his arrogance and determination to achieve LAW & ORDER!

His verbal assault threw into raw, sharp relief his self-righteous mission to sterilize society from the infection which I obviously am. Fueled by years of action movies, Dragnet reruns, subliminal white supremacy propaganda, discount beer, anabolic steroids, doughnuts, and patriotic emotionalism, our fine young officer is perfectly suited to the task assigned to him by the powers that be.

To maintain terror, to create divisions in the community, and to cultivate "enemies", and insure maintenance of power through techniques of "divide and conquer", thus perpetuating a crime and punishment based economy in the service of leaders whose objectives he cannot understand.

And we are the enemy. We are the stain on his flat, two dimensional, colorless world. We are the ungrateful ward, and threatening prey.

His clear, pure hatred of us is not just taught to him; indoctrinated from birth. It's a part of his very being, written in large capital letters on his DNA. And at the core of it all is a focal point of self hatred and guilt for all he has done, all he thinks, all he is,

And he's going to make us pay for it if it costs him his last breath.

Or maybe he's just having a bad day? After all, it is hot outside, and he has to walk around in that bulky uniform. People giving him attitudes all night.

Abruptly he leaves, he seems nervous.

Seconds later my acquaintance bids me farewell, and I'm left with the realization that not once during the cop's diatribe did he look me in the eye. He barely acknowledged my existence.

I walked away.

Later I went to the Blue Note for the jam session. I sounded terrible: I didn't feel like playing.

Autumn in New York

A cool still invitation to the secrets of the night wraps me in its silent embrace. Colors are sharper, the air is cleaner. Sounds in this world share tales of distant life.

The heavier clothing of this season a fortress and shield; comfort in the absence of the sun's warmth.

Windows give glimpses into restaurants and homes. Promises of hearty food and warm sanctuary among embracing furniture and dark wood from the bite of cold winds float by.

The indigent shuffle past comforts denied them. Lights from distant skyscrapers insult their pain.

But I have my own comfort and my own pain. Don't ask; I will not explain. Would you understand if I tried?

Each sight, each smell, and each breath of wind sings its song of praise; and brings from its resting place memories of years past. Treasures sacred to none but I.

The night wears on. It's rhythm driving to its inevitable end. The clubs close, people go home, or to new destinations, chasing the eternal party they'll never really find.

Early risers walk tired and stiff to their jobs; small groups congregate in doorways and loading docks. Drinking dishwater flavored coffee from blue paper cups that exclaim "It's our pleasure to serve you", and sharing a moment of peaceful camaraderie before their work begins.

Stars fade, the moon relinquishes it's domination of the sky. The eastern sky reluctantly gives up its indigo for an ever brightening blue. The cool, still night soon to be a memory as the sun takes its rightful claim.

All praise and gratitude is due to Allah for the gift of this night. Its beauty and music are a gift I accept with humility. The November morning is here.

Autumn in New York - it's good to live it again.

On This Night

On this night, the world is pregnant with Light and Beauty,

I ask the stars "To what will she give birth?"

Their answer reverberated through the universe.

"Say nothing, just be!"

When the strings of my instrument shall offer her uncorrupted
spirit,

In my heart a sweeter sound shall sing,

Bursting through my expanded breast,

Divining realities beyond the veils of our eyes.

My Undefinable Lover beckons to me:

"Return; even if you broke your vows a thousand times!

Bear these trials patiently.

Soon you will know."

On this night, how can I refuse such an invitation?
How shall I deny such a sadaqah?

My Beloved is rich and I am impoverished.

My Beloved needs nothing,

I need my Beloved.

Even so, the forgetfulness that is written within my flesh, diverts me.

On this night, I built a fire, and sat near it for warmth.

A moth flew toward it.

It glided as close to the flames as it dared.

It was so in love with the light;

it didn't care if it was destroyed;

it had to reach its Beloved.

The moth almost flew away

to return to its tribe to tell them

of the wondrous light it had fallen in love with.

But it could not leave its Beloved.

It dove headlong into union and was consumed.

I wept bitterly with shame and remorse:

That moth was a better Muslim than I am!

Another True story.

Once upon a time, I was walking to an appointment in New York City. When I passed the corner of Canal Street and Sixth Avenue, I saw a Monarch Butterfly!

I asked it "What on Earth are you doing here"?

It just smiled, and flew away.

Shut up, Dawoud.

We are stars.

Grains of gold dust waiting at the event horizon of an ocean of time.

My heart beats like a pendulum of love.

The songs that escape my lips are rapturous sighs of eternalness.

Let all things drop into this ocean.

Let us die each moment.

Let us be born each moment.

Oh we who cry "But,,," and roar "And,,,,"

And bought a book of lies for an exorbitant price,

We see only ourselves.

Where did our innocence flee when we "grew up?"

Where does our certain knowledge go when we die?

Ya Allah! I'm tangled in abstracts!

I've said too much!

Time to be silent.

ABOUT THE AUTHOR:

Dawoud Kringle is a New York City based musician, writer, and artist. If music could be defined, it would be World Jazz Electronica Fusion. It's a jazz experience from an other-worldly realm, with a Downbeat / electronica edge; and his work on the sitar and dilruba earned a reputation as 'The Jimi Hendrix of the sitar.' He has performed in the US and Europe, appeared on many recordings, composed for film, theater, and dance performances, and conducts music meditation sessions, wherein he guides group meditation using musical form and sound.

Kringle is an accomplished writer / novelist who writes for several online publications, wrote a Sufi Science Fiction novel A QUANTUM HIJRA (publsihed by Leilha Publications). His first book has been compared to Dune and Shrodigger's Cat, and is, in the realm of Islam influenced science fiction, considered unique. His second release, A MANSION WITH MANY ROOMS is a collection of short stories and poetry that explore the multidimensional spiritualism of Islam / Sufism from a new perspective. Another Sufi science fiction novel and a textbook on music are in the works. His visual art works have been displayed at openings such as the event ON THE INNER AND OUTER WORLDS; curated by Openings Collective, and hosted at the Church of St. Paul the Apostle in NYC. His works grace the covers of A QUANTUM HIJRA and A MANSION WITH MANY ROOMS.